CARDBOARD ROCKETS TO SPACE

T.C. Annas

TABLE OF CONTENTS

Dedication ....*i*

Chapter 1: Neil's Dream Takes Flight 1

Chapter 2: Grandpa's Inspiring Words 4

Chapter 3: Building the Impossible Spaceship 8

Chapter 4: Schoolyard Challenges.. 12

Chapter 5: The First Test Flight 16

Chapter 6: Research and Discovery...................................... 20

Chapter 7: Overcoming Obstacles 23

Chapter 8: The Power of Imagination 27

Chapter 9: A New Perspective 31

Chapter 10: Sharing his Passion 36

Chapter 11: The School Science Fair.................................... 40

Chapter 12: Unexpected Friendship 43

Chapter 13: Facing Criticism.. 47

Chapter 14: Expanding Horizons 50

Chapter 15: A New Challenge... 54

Chapter 16: The Design Process... 58

Chapter 17: Seeking Mentorship 62

Chapter 18: Technical Difficulties.. 67

Chapter 19: Celebrating Small Victories 71

Chapter 20: A Breakthrough 75

Chapter 21: Sharing his Success... 79

Chapter 22: Community Support 83

Chapter 23: Overcoming Self-Doubt 87

Chapter 24: Embracing Uniqueness 91

Chapter 25: Inspiring Others 95

Chapter 26: The Final Launch 98

Chapter 27: Reflecting on the Journey 102

Chapter 28: Celebrating Success 105

Chapter 29: Future Aspirations 109

Chapter 30: The Enduring Power of Dreams 113

Acknowledgments 117

Author Biography 118

DEDICATION

This book is dedicated to every child who has ever dared to dream big, no matter the size of their hands, the length of their arms, or the whispers of doubt that may surround them. It is dedicated to those who find strength in their differences, who transform perceived limitations into stepping stones of ingenuity, and who understand that true success is not just about reaching the destination, but about the incredible journey to get there.

This story is for the young Neil's within us all. The ones who gaze at the stars with wide-eyed wonder, who build magnificent castles from cardboard boxes, who find joy in the simplest of things, and who never cease to believe in the power of their own unique dreams.

It is dedicated to the grandpas and grandmas, parents and teachers, friends and mentors, who offer unwavering support, encouragement, and the kindling of belief needed to ignite the flames of a child's aspirations. Those who provide the safe space for dreams to take flight, for imaginations to soar, and for creativity to blossom. Those who see the extraordinary potential within every child, regardless of their perceived imperfections.

This book is also a dedication to the quiet strength and unwavering spirit of those who have faced adversity with resilience and grace, who have found inventive solutions to life's challenges, and who have proven that limitations are often merely perceptions, overcome by determination and an unyielding belief in oneself. May this story serve as a reminder that our differences are not weaknesses, but sources of unique strength and perspective. May it inspire us all to embrace our individuality, to celebrate our uniqueness, and to pursue our dreams with unwavering passion, creativity, and courage.

To those who believe in the impossible, to those who find the extraordinary in the ordinary, to those who nurture the dreams of children, and to every child who dares to reach for the stars:

this book is for you. May it remind you that the journey itself, filled with challenges overcome, is the truest measure of triumph. May it ignite within you the unwavering belief that your dreams, however impossible they may seem, are worth pursuing. And may it inspire you to always reach for the stars, one creative, determined step at a time.

CHAPTER 1:

NEIL'S DREAM TAKES FLIGHT

Neil's small town was nestled beside a vast, starlit canvas. Every night, as the sun dipped below the horizon, painting the sky in fiery hues of orange and purple, Neil would find himself drawn to his window. He wasn't just looking; he was imagining. He saw swirling galaxies, distant gas clouds, and the silvery gleam of the moon, a celestial beacon that seemed to call him towards the unknown.

His room, a sanctuary of dreams, reflected this fascination. Posters of planets, brave astronauts, and gleaming rockets adorned every wall, a vibrant tapestry woven from his boundless imagination. Books on astronomy, carefully marked up in his own handwriting, lined his shelves. His fingers, three on his right hand, expertly turned the pages, their movements a testament to his dexterity and determination.

His shorter arm, a physical difference he had learned to accept as part of himself, never hindered his ability to understand a concept or handle an object. It was a challenge, certainly, but one he had learned to overcome with ingenuity and resolve. He meticulously crafted miniature rockets from recycled materials such as cardboard tubes that became rocket bodies, bottle caps were repurposed as nozzles and old toy parts transformed into intricate control panels. Each spaceship was a testament to his craftsmanship and dedication, a tiny universe built from scraps and dreams.

His family played a pivotal role in nurturing his dreams. His parents, although initially concerned about the realities of his ambitions, were always supportive, encouraging his curiosity and providing the resources he needed.

His mother spent hours reading him captivating stories about space exploration, filling his mind with fantastical adventures and courageous pioneers. His father, a skilled craftsman himself, taught him how to work with tools, adapting his instructions to suit Neil's unique hand, showing him that limitations could be worked around with a bit of thought and patience.

But it was his grandfather, a retired engineer with a twinkle in his eye and a heart full of wisdom, who became Neil's most steadfast champion. Grandpa, a man whose own life had been shaped by perseverance, understood the importance of nurturing a child's dreams. He would spend countless hours sharing stories from his youth. Tales of setbacks and success, near misses and proud victories.

He would often say, "Neil, my boy, the greatest adventures aren't always the easiest, but they're always the most rewarding. Never let anyone tell you what you can't achieve."

Grandpa's words resonated deeply with Neil. He instilled in him the belief that perceived limitations were mere obstacles, to be overcome with ingenuity and unwavering determination. He showed Neil how challenges could be tackled bit by bit, how tough problems were solved not by force but with clever thinking and steady work. He taught Neil patience, how to adapt, and the importance of asking for help when needed.

These evening chats, surrounded by the warmth of their home, filled with the smell of freshly baked cookies and Grandpa's low, steady voice, became a cornerstone of Neil's childhood. They weren't just stories, they were lessons, blueprints for how to build his future. Through Grandpa's eyes, Neil saw a world where the word "impossible" just meant "not yet tried."

Even the simple things in daily life became a chance for Neil to show his adaptability. Buttoning a shirt might take longer, but he'd figured out a method. A set of movements that worked for him. Tying shoelaces was tricky, but he made it happen, his smaller hand gripping with surprising strength and control.

These small victories mirrored the bigger challenges he faced chasing his dream, each one reinforcing that his difference wasn't a barrier, it was just a different way of doing things.

He used that difference to spark his creativity. Neil adapted tools and invented techniques to handle delicate materials. He even built a custom workbench, fitted to his height and hand size. His bedroom wasn't just where he slept, it was his lab, his workshop, a launchpad for ideas powered by dreams, and Grandpa's quiet encouragement.

Neil's determination didn't stop at his doorstep. At school, he faced tests of a different kind. While many classmates were fascinated by his spaceship models and comprehensive space knowledge, some didn't quite get him. A few teased him now and then, not out of cruelty, but ignorance.

Neil never let their words knock him down. Instead, he used those moments to share his passion. He'd explain how rockets worked, why stars twinkled, or what it felt like to imagine walking on Mars. Slowly, even the skeptics started listening. Some even became curious admirers and asked to help with his models.

Instead, he used these encounters as an opportunity to share his knowledge and enthusiasm, often converting skeptics into curious admirers.

His perspective, shaped by his family's support and Grandpa's guidance, became his greatest strength. He didn't see his physical difference as a flaw. It was a different lens, one that made him inventive, patient, and bold.

Neil showed again and again that the real limits weren't in our bodies, they were in the doubts people believed. He was proof that what made you different could be exactly what made you strong.

Neil's journey was only just beginning, but his path was clear; driven by dreams, lifted by imagination, and steered by love and wisdom.

The stars were waiting. Neil, with every part of himself, was ready to go meet them.

CHAPTER 2:

GRANDPA'S INSPIRING WORDS

The aroma of freshly baked oatmeal cookies filled the air, a comforting scent that always seemed to accompany Grandpa's storytelling sessions. Neil, nestled in his favorite armchair, a worn, plush thing that had seen countless nights of shared laughter and whispered dreams, listened closely. Outside, the wind whistled a gentle tune, a counterpoint to the rhythmic crackling of the fire in the hearth. The scene was idyllic, a perfect setting for the tales Grandpa was about to share.

Tonight's stories weren't about faraway galaxies or intrepid astronauts. They were about Grandpa himself, about a young man with big dreams and even bigger challenges. He spoke of his early days as an engineering apprentice, of working long hours in a bustling workshop, surrounded by the clang of metal and the whir of machinery. He described the intricate designs he'd wrestled with, the complex equations he'd painstakingly solved, and the moments of sheer frustration that had tested his limits.

You see, Neil," Grandpa began, his voice a low rumble that carried a lifetime's worth of experience, "I wasn't always this seasoned engineer you know. I started out just like you—full of dreams, ideas buzzing in my head—but facing hurdles that felt way too big sometimes." He chuckled, a warm, comforting sound. "One of my first major projects was designing a bridge for a small, remote village. The specifications were demanding, the terrain challenging, and the resources... well, let's just say they were limited."

He described the meticulous planning involved, the countless hours spent poring over blueprints, the seemingly endless calculations, and the countless setbacks. He spoke of nights spent staring at diagrams, wrestling with equations that refused to yield answers and the gnawing doubt that had crept into his mind. "There were times," he admitted, "when I felt utterly defeated. I questioned my abilities, wondered if I was up to the task. The bridge seemed an impossible dream."

But then, Grandpa's voice took on a stronger, more determined tone. He described how he'd broken the massive project down into smaller, more manageable tasks. He explained how he'd sought advice from experienced colleagues, how he'd spent hours researching alternative solutions, and how he'd relentlessly pursued each challenge, never allowing himself to be completely discouraged. "It wasn't about being the best or the brightest, Neil," he emphasized, "it was about sticking with it. Finding smart workarounds. Not giving up just because things looked too hard."

He spoke of a particularly difficult problem; a crucial structural part that refused to fit within the budget and available materials. He'd spent sleepless nights trying to find a solution, poring over textbooks and engineering manuals, until he stumbled upon an innovative design in a decades-old publication. It wasn't the most straightforward approach, but it was the most effective, and it allowed him to complete the bridge successfully, within budget and on time. He'd proved, through sheer determination and innovative thinking, that perceived limitations were often self-imposed.

Grandpa recounted other challenges, a collapsed scaffolding during construction, a sudden storm that threatened to delay the project, and a miscalculation that nearly caused a fatal accident. Each challenge was met with resourcefulness, patience, and an unwavering belief in his abilities. He didn't shy away from recounting his mistakes; instead, he used them as learning experiences, highlighting the importance of admitting errors and using them to refine his skills.

"Every setback," he said, his eyes twinkling, "became a lesson, a stepping stone towards success. You learn more from your failures than you do from your victories, Neil. It's how you bounce back that shows what you're really made of." He paused, taking a sip of his tea, before continuing.

He then shared stories of his later career, designing innovative energy-efficient systems, creating groundbreaking safety protocols, and working on projects that pushed the boundaries of engineering.

Each story highlighted the importance of careful planning, resourcefulness, and the power of collaboration. He spoke of working with a team of talented individuals, each bringing their unique skills and abilities to the table, showing the strength of teamwork and the value of seeking help when needed.

Grandpa's stories weren't just tales of engineering triumphs. They were parables of perseverance, resilience, and the power of the human spirit to overcome adversity. He showed Neil that difficulties were not roadblocks but opportunities for growth, and challenges to be overcome with creativity and determination. He emphasized the importance of breaking down large, daunting tasks into smaller, achievable goals, celebrating each small victory along the way.

As the fire crackled and the wind howled softly outside, Grandpa's voice filled the room, painting vivid pictures of his past, weaving a narrative of inspiration and hope. Neil listened, captivated, not just by the stories themselves, but by the underlying message: that perceived limitations were nothing more than obstacles, and that with enough perseverance and ingenuity, even the most ambitious dreams were attainable. Grandpa didn't preach; he showed, through his own experiences, that success was not about talent alone, but about the unwavering spirit of pursuing one's goals, despite the setbacks and challenges.

Neil understood that Grandpa wasn't just sharing his career achievements; he was passing on a legacy. A legacy of unwavering determination, relentless pursuit, and the belief that every individual, regardless of their physical capabilities, has the potential to achieve great things. It wasn't just about reaching for the stars; it was about the journey itself, the obstacles overcome, and the lessons learned along the way.

The aroma of the cookies mingled with the scent of Grandpa's pipe tobacco, a familiar and comforting fragrance that signified shared moments of wisdom and encouragement. As the night deepened, and the stories concluded, Neil felt a surge of renewed determination. He wasn't just dreaming of space; he was preparing for the journey. He understood now, more clearly than ever, that the path wouldn't be easy, but it would be his path, fueled by perseverance, ingenuity, and the unwavering belief in himself, a belief instilled in him by his wise grandfather. The stars, twinkling brightly outside, seemed to wink in approval, their distant light reflecting the bright spark of hope ignited within Neil's heart. He had his dream, and he had the courage, inspired by his Grandpa's words, to chase it. The journey to the stars, while daunting, had become a little less distant, a little less impossible.

CHAPTER 3:

BUILDING THE IMPOSSIBLE SPACESHIP

The next morning, armed with a renewed sense of purpose, Neil embarked on his most ambitious project yet: building his impossible spaceship. Grandpa's tales of engineering challenges resonated deeply within him, fueling his determination. He didn't need a sleek, futuristic spacecraft built from expensive materials; he needed a vessel born from ingenuity, flexibility, and his own belief in what he could do. His spaceship would be a testament to his spirit, a symbol of his dreams taking flight.

His quest began in the familiar landscape of his own backyard, a treasure trove of discarded materials waiting to be transformed. Old cardboard boxes, once destined for the recycling bin, now held the potential to become the hull of his magnificent vessel. Bottle caps, gleaming with iridescent colors in the sunlight, would become rivets and intricate details. Broken toys, casualties of playtime battles, found new life as control panels and propulsion systems.

Each piece, carefully selected and meticulously examined, whispered tales of potential and transformation, mirroring the journey Neil himself was about to undertake.

This three-fingered hand, often perceived as a limitation, became his greatest asset. It forced him to think differently, to find creative solutions others might overlook. Where some might reach for glue, Neil used precisely crafted clips and fasteners, fashioned from repurposed wire and discarded metal pieces. His smaller hand, nimble and precise, allowed him to work with intricate details that larger hands might struggle with. He even discovered ways to use his hand's unique configuration to create remarkably sturdy and surprisingly aerodynamic structures from cardboard, forming curves and angles that would've been nearly impossible using conventional techniques. His workspace became a canvas of creativity, a testament to his resourcefulness.

The local library became his second home, a sanctuary of knowledge and inspiration. Surrounded by towering shelves filled with books on engineering, aerospace, and science fiction, Neil immersed himself in the world of spaceship design. He devoured blueprints of iconic spacecraft, studying their intricate layouts and marveling at the inventiveness of their creators. He researched rocket propulsion, orbital mechanics, and the complexities of space travel, his drive to overcome every obstacle fueled by Grandpa's stories.

The library's vast collection of technical manuals became his guiding stars. He wasn't just reading; he was understanding, absorbing, and applying the principles he learned to his own unique creation. He explored different propulsion systems, comparing the strengths and weaknesses of chemical rockets, ion thrusters, and even theoretical warp drives. He spent hours poring over diagrams of spacecraft control systems, studying how sensors, actuators, and computers worked together. He began sketching his own designs, mixing innovative ideas with the knowledge he'd gained from the books.

The process wasn't without its challenges. There were moments of frustration when creations didn't work as planned, when pieces refused to align, or when the glue simply wouldn't stick. Instead of giving up, Neil saw these as learning moments. He documented his failures, analyzed what went wrong, and brainstormed new approaches. He learned from every mistake, refining his techniques, and came out each time with a deeper understanding of engineering and design. Each failure strengthened his resolve, pushing him to innovate, adapt, and keep going.

The library's staff, noticing Neil's dedication and focus, became his unexpected allies. Mrs. Gable, the kind librarian with a warm smile and a love for old science fiction novels, became a mentor, giving him access to rare books and technical resources. She praised his persistence, offering words of support that lifted his spirits during tougher days. She even helped him find some specialized materials like a stronger adhesive, thin metal sheets, and tiny light bulbs for his control panel, adding polish and possibility to his extraordinary project.

As weeks turned into months, Neil's spaceship began to take shape. The cardboard boxes, carefully cut and layered, formed a sturdy, aerodynamic hull. The bottle caps, secured with precisely crafted clips, added texture and a touch of futuristic flair. The broken toys, repurposed and reimagined, became control panels, navigation systems, and even a miniature, gravity-defying model of a lunar rover. His spaceship was no ordinary model; it was a monument to creativity, resilience, and the belief that anything is possible if you really commit to it.

The spaceship wasn't just a physical creation, it was a journey of self-discovery. Every challenge overcome brought Neil closer to understanding what he was capable of. He learned that limits were often self-imposed and that with enough perseverance, anything could be achieved. The process sharpened his problem-solving skills, strengthened his critical thinking, and gave him a real sense of confidence.

He meticulously documented his progress in a detailed journal, sketching diagrams, jotting down calculations, and recording both triumphs and setbacks. This journal became more than a record of building; it became a personal map of growth, a reflection of his resilience, and a celebration of how he saw the world. He realized his three-fingered hand wasn't a hindrance at all, it was part of what made his approach unique. It forced him to design differently, to solve problems in ways others wouldn't even think of.

As the spaceship neared completion, a sense of anticipation filled Neil. This wasn't just a model. It was a real, physical representation of his dream. A symbol of his perseverance and belief in himself. It was a symbol of his journey, his determination, and his ability to overcome challenges. He had turned discarded scraps into a magnificent vessel, powered not by fuel but by creativity and determination. The final touches, the tiny lights in the control panel, the carefully placed navigation system were done with precision and care, infused with the same spirit Grandpa's stories had always carried.

The spaceship, when completed, was a remarkable sight. It wasn't perfect in the traditional sense—it wasn't sleek or factory-made—but it was perfect because it was Neil's. A blend of salvaged materials, inventive design, and unstoppable drive. It stood as a symbol of his grit, a beacon of hope pointing toward his future. It was proof that limitations only exist if you let them. The stars, gleaming outside his window, seemed to shine a little brighter, as if they recognized what he had built. The impossible spaceship was finished. And with it, the real journey had begun.

Chapter 4:

Schoolyard Challenges

The school bell's shrill ring shattered the quiet concentration Neil had found amidst the towering shelves of the library. He carefully closed his journal, a record of his spaceship's progress and his own burgeoning self-discovery, and tucked it safely into his backpack. As he walked out, the late afternoon sun cast long shadows across the schoolyard, painting the scene in hues of orange and purple. The familiar loudness of children's laughter and shouts washed over him as he stepped onto the playground.

It wasn't always a welcoming sound. For Neil, the schoolyard was a miniature copy of the wider world, a place where his differences were often magnified, where his passion for space sometimes drew unwanted attention. He'd learned to navigate the complexities of social interaction, to understand the nuances of acceptance and rejection, the delicate balance between confidence and vulnerability.

Today, however, was different. The successful completion of the impossible spaceship had imbued him with a newfound confidence, a quiet strength that radiated from within. He felt a sense of pride, not just in his accomplishment, but in his ability to face challenges head-on. His gait, usually slightly hesitant, was now more assured. He carried himself with a quiet dignity, a subtle self-assurance that seemed to change the way people perceived him.

As he approached his usual spot beneath the old oak tree, a group of boys were gathered, their voices a mixture of taunts and laughter. He recognized some of them from his class: Mark, with his perpetually messy hair; Kevin, always quick with a sarcastic remark; and Jason, who seemed to revel in the attention he gained from instigating trouble.

Their attention was focused on something small and wriggling in Mark's hand, a grasshopper. Their laughter sounded cruel, even from a distance.

Neil usually avoided such encounters, opting for the solitude of the library or the quiet creativity of his backyard workshop. Today, however, something within him felt different. He felt a quiet strength, a resilience forged in the fires of his own challenges. He walked towards the group, his head held high, his shoulders squared.

As he approached, their laughter ceased, replaced by a moment of uncomfortable silence. Mark, noticing Neil, quickly stuffed the grasshopper into his pocket. Kevin, ever the instigator, tried to break the silence with a snide remark.

"Look who it is, the space cadet," he sneered, his voice dripping with sarcasm.

Jason echoed the taunt, adding a crude imitation of Neil's slightly awkward gait.

Neil, instead of reacting defensively, paused, his gaze steady. He didn't flinch under their scrutiny. Instead, he calmly opened his backpack, carefully extracting a small, meticulously crafted model rocket. It was one of his earlier creations, smaller than the impossibly complex spaceship, but still a testament to his ingenuity. He held it up, the afternoon sun catching the glint of the bottle-cap fins.

"This," he said, his voice calm but firm, "is a model of a sounding rocket. It uses a solid propellant motor to reach a considerable altitude."

He paused, letting his words hang in the air, the weight of his knowledge subtly shifting the dynamic. He continued, his tone lifting, adding a touch of enthusiasm.

"Did you know the most powerful rocket ever built—the Saturn V—was three hundred and sixty-three feet tall and could lift over six million pounds into space? It took thousands of engineers and scientists years of planning and some serious innovation to make it happen."

Their taunts were silenced. Their eyes, initially filled with mockery, widened slightly, their expressions shifting from amusement to a hint of curiosity. Neil's passion, his depth of knowledge, had captured their attention. He continued to explain the intricate workings of rocket propulsion, the challenges of space travel, and the wonder of exploring the cosmos. He spoke with an authority that belied his age, his words infused with a quiet enthusiasm that drew them in.

Mark, the usually disruptive one, was the first to break the silence.

"Whoa," he whispered, eyes wide with wonder.

Kevin, too, was listening, his usual sarcasm replaced with real interest. Even Jason, hesitant at first, seemed caught up in what Neil was saying.

Neil, sensing their shift in attitude, kept going. He skillfully wove in stories of astronauts, planetary exploration, and the marvels of the universe. He showed them detailed sketches from his journal, explaining the design principles behind his creations and the innovative solutions he'd come up with to tackle challenges. He broke down the aerodynamic features of his spaceship's design and talked through the careful engineering behind his rocket models.

His unique approach, shaped by finding creative solutions with his three-fingered hand, became a source of fascination. He showed them how he'd adapted, how what seemed like a limitation had turned into a strength. His face lit up with passion, and his hands moved animatedly as he spoke. He had turned the schoolyard into a classroom, transforming what could've been a painful moment into a chance to share what he loved and open minds.

The afternoon sun began to dip below the horizon as Neil's impromptu lesson came to a close. The group remained gathered around, their earlier mockery replaced by genuine respect. Mark, still holding onto the grasshopper, asked a surprisingly detailed question about orbital mechanics. Kevin, unexpectedly earnest, asked if Neil could help with his science project. Even Jason muttered that Neil's spaceship was "pretty cool."

The experience was deeply fulfilling for Neil. He had not only managed a tricky social moment; he had used his knowledge and passion to change minds. He turned potential teasing into curiosity, and curiosity into connection. He realized his differences weren't something to hide, but something that made him stronger. The bell rang again, marking the end of the day, but everything felt different now. The usual unease of the schoolyard had softened.

He walked home with a lighter step, carrying not just the pride of building a spaceship, but the quiet satisfaction of having reached someone. He had overcome more than a physical challenge today; he had pushed through a social one too, proving that his resilience and spirit were just as powerful as his intellect.

The stars were still out there, waiting for him. But now, he knew he wasn't entirely alone in reaching for them. He had found unexpected allies, and the road ahead, though still full of challenges, seemed a little less steep. The impossible was still possible. And he was ready.

Chapter 5:

The First Test Flight

The final piece, a minuscule antenna fashioned from a bent paperclip, clicked into place. Neil stepped back, admiring his creation. It wasn't just a model; it was a testament to perseverance, a tangible representation of his dreams. The spaceship, impossibly complex in its miniature form, gleamed under the afternoon sun, a beacon of hope in his small backyard workshop. He'd spent weeks, months, even, meticulously crafting each part, overcoming the challenges presented by his three-fingered hand with ingenious solutions. He'd learned to manipulate tiny wires with surprising dexterity, to weld delicate parts with unwavering patience, to build a structure that defied the limitations of its size.

A wave of emotion washed over him: pride, relief, and a touch of nervousness. Tomorrow was the day. The day he would share his achievement, not just with his grandpa, but with his friends, his teachers, even the skeptical eyes of his classmates. Tomorrow was the day of the first test flight.

He carefully placed the spaceship into a protective case, lining it with soft foam to prevent any damage. He checked his meticulously compiled notes one last time, ensuring he hadn't missed any crucial detail. The launch sequence, the trajectory calculations, the expected impact; every element was meticulously planned, each step carefully considered. This wasn't just a child's game; this was a meticulously planned mission.

That night, sleep eluded him. Excitement thrummed through him, a vibrant energy that kept him tossing and turning in bed. He imagined the scene: the expectant faces of his friends, the curious gaze of his teachers, the proud smile of his grandpa. He pictured the spaceship hurtling down the grassy slope, a miniature rocket defying gravity, carrying not just itself, but the weight of his dreams. He also imagined the possibility of failure; the spaceship might not roll as planned, the landing might be bumpy, or perhaps, worse, the whole thing could collapse. Yet the thought only fueled his determinationHe would face whatever came his way.

The next morning dawned bright and clear, the perfect day for a launch. He woke up with a nervous energy, a mixture of excitement and apprehension that kept him on his toes. After a hearty breakfast prepared by his grandpa, they set off for the town park, the spaceship carefully nestled in his backpack. He had selected a location away from the crowds, hoping for a bit of privacy amidst the celebration. He had invited his friends Mark, Kevin, and Jason, who seemed much friendlier now, plus his teachers and any curious passers-by.

The park was bustling with activity, but Neil found a quiet corner near a gently sloping hill, perfect for his "launchpad." He laid out a small checkered picnic blanket, the ideal staging area for his momentous event. His grandpa, beaming with pride, helped him unpack the spaceship and set up a small video camera to record the occasion. He had a short speech prepared to mark the day.

As Neil's friends and teachers gathered, a murmur of anticipation rippled through the crowd. Mark, Kevin, and Jason, their earlier skepticism replaced with genuine curiosity, crowded around, eyes wide as Neil explained the intricacies of his design and the challenges he'd overcome. He described the hours of meticulous work, the late nights perfecting every detail, the innovative solutions he'd devised to compensate for his physical limitations. He spoke with quiet confidence, his words carrying a conviction that silenced any lingering doubt.

Neil then delivered his brief speech, his voice clear and strong despite the nerves. He talked about his dreams, his journey, the unwavering support of his grandpa, and the importance of believing in oneself, no matter the odds. He spoke of perseverance, the rewards of hard work, and the joy of pursuing passions. He mentioned his teachers, explaining how they had encouraged him and never doubted him. His words resonated with the small crowd, their initial amusement and skepticism replaced by admiration and respect. Even the park's caretaker, an old man who often grumbled about children's games, watched with a wistful smile.

Finally, the moment arrived. Neil carefully placed his spaceship at the top of the gentle slope, its miniature solar panels glinting under the sun. He took a deep breath, excitement and nervousness mingling. He released the spaceship, and it rolled smoothly down the hill, its tiny wheels barely making a sound. It rolled on, perfectly, following the precise route Neil had planned. It never toppled and reached the end untouched.

The crowd erupted in cheers, their applause echoing through the park. Neil's heart swelled with joy, a feeling far beyond anything he had imagined. The "test flight" was no spectacular launch, no fiery exhaust plume, no soaring arc through the air. Yet the simple roll down a hill had come to mean something much greater: a symbol of Neil's determination, his ability to overcome challenges, and the enduring power of dreams.

More than that, it was a testament to the unwavering support of his community. His friends, his teachers, his grandpa—each had played a crucial role, contributing in their own way to his success. The event turned a seemingly simple act into a powerful reminder of what can be achieved when dreams are nurtured.

The first nervousness that had gripped Neil melted away, replaced by a quiet sense of accomplishment and profound gratitude.

The video of the launch, later shared with the school, became a source of inspiration, highlighting the power of believing in oneself and pursuing aspirations. Neil's story reached other students, many dealing with challenges of their own. He wasn't just the boy who built a spaceship; he became a beacon of hope, proving that limitations do not define potential.

As the sun began to set, casting long shadows across the park, Neil stood beside his grandpa, a gentle smile on his face. He looked up, the first stars flickering into view. His journey had only just begun, but he knew he was ready for whatever lay ahead. The test flight was merely the beginning. He had shown his abilities, and more importantly, the people around him believed in his skills too. The journey had only started.

CHAPTER 6:

RESEARCH AND DISCOVERY

The success of the model spaceship launch fueled Neil's passion even further. The cheers of his friends, the pride in his grandpa's eyes, and the respectful admiration of his teachers had ignited a fire within him, a desire to delve even deeper into the science behind his dream. The simple roll down the hill wasn't just a successful test; it was a stepping stone, pushing him toward a more profound understanding of space exploration.

His next mission wasn't about building another model, it was about understanding the very principles that governed space travel. His journey led him to the town library, a majestic building filled with the quiet whispers of countless stories and the silent wisdom of accumulated knowledge. The library, previously a place for occasional visits, had now become his sanctuary, a place where discovery came to life.

He began with the basics, devouring children's books on astronomy, captivated by the breathtaking images of planets swirling with vibrant hues, nebulae painted across the cosmos like celestial brushstrokes, and galaxies spiraling into infinity. He learned about the constellations, tracing their shimmering patterns across the night sky, each star a distant sun, each planet a possible world waiting to be explored.

His first explorations expanded quickly. Soon, he was venturing into more complex texts, tackling books on astrophysics with a fervor that surprised even himself. The daunting equations and intricate diagrams didn't deter him; instead, they challenged him, sparking his curiosity and pushing him to learn more. He meticulously copied diagrams, carefully annotating each step, each equation, every important concept. He sought out patterns, connections, and underlying principles, turning complicated ideas into something he could slowly piece together.

Neil discovered that his three-fingered hand, once seen as a limitation, became an unexpected advantage. The dexterity he had developed building his spaceship translated into a new way of working with books. He learned to flip pages with surprising grace, to hold open heavy volumes with a unique grip, and to highlight key passages with impressive precision. His limitations had shaped the way he approached problems, and now, he was using those skills to unravel some of the universe's biggest questions.

His unique perspective helped him notice patterns and links others might have missed. He found elegance in what first seemed like chaos, the balance of gravity and inertia, the subtle rules of celestial movement. He began to connect different areas of science, physics, chemistry, and math, understanding how they worked together to explain how space travel was even possible.

He wasn't just reading, he was imagining. He pictured himself flying through space, piloting a craft past constellations he now knew by name. He imagined walking across the dusty red surface of Mars, his breath fogging in the helmet. He felt the light tug of lunar gravity, the weightlessness of orbit, the endless sweep of the galaxy stretching before him.

The library became more than a building. It was a portal to other worlds, a launchpad for his imagination. He spent hours there, surrounded by books, breathing in the scent of old paper and leather, the quiet hum of the place matching the pace of his always-whirring thoughts. The librarian, a kind woman with a warm smile and a love of facts, became his guide. She pointed him toward the right shelves, recommended books, and cheered his progress.

But books weren't his only source. He dove into documentaries, online articles, and NASA websites. He soaked up everything, the history of space travel, from Sputnik to Apollo, and the missions of modern-day rovers exploring distant planets. He followed active missions, studying their launch paths, tracking spacecraft as they drifted through the solar system. He learned about international space agencies, their technologies, and the problems they were trying to solve. He kept a running timeline of major space missions and what each one had discovered.

He also explored the ethical and philosophical sides of space exploration. He learned about the search for life beyond Earth, the importance of peaceful space use, and the need to protect the environments we explore. He even chatted with the librarian about space politics and international teamwork. It gave him a bigger picture, one that included not just science and tech, but values and responsibility too.

He studied different rocket types, how their engines worked, and what it takes to survive space. He looked at the materials used for building spacecraft, how control systems operate, and what astronauts need to stay alive on long missions. He even started sketching out new ideas, wondering how future spacecraft might be built.

But Neil's journey wasn't a solo mission. He shared everything he learned with his friends. Their curiosity grew. They helped him build models, draw diagrams, and ask bigger questions. Mark, good with numbers, helped solve equations. Kevin, who loved to draw, illustrated planets and rocket designs. Jason, always into gadgets, kept up with new space tech and helped with research.

Neil's growing knowledge didn't just stay in space. He used science to solve real-life problems, fixing a broken bike, organizing his books more efficiently, even helping classmates with tricky homework. His teachers noticed. His confidence grew.

The library, part classroom, part headquarters, part dream launchpad, had helped him transform. It gave him more than knowledge; it gave him direction, a passion, a reason to keep learning. What once felt like a far-off dream was slowly turning into a real path forward, powered by curiosity, determination, and the people who believed in him.

The boy who once saw his difference as a barrier was now exploring the stars, bit by bit. And his journey was only just beginning. He knew what came next, not just another model, but something far more ambitious, a clear mission statement that captured everything he hoped to build and discover.

CHAPTER 7:

OVERCOMING OBSTACLES

The first excitement of his successful model launch quickly gave way to a new set of challenges. His next ambition was far more ambitious: a model spaceship capable of not just rolling downhill, but of launching itself using a miniature rocket engine. This presented a whole new level of complexity. He needed to design a propulsion system, a stable launch platform, and a control mechanism, all on a miniature scale.

His three-fingered hand, once a source of self-doubt, became his greatest ally. The fine motor skills he'd developed over years of crafting intricate models allowed him to manipulate tiny components with surprising dexterity. Where others might have struggled, he found inventive solutions. He devised a unique gripping technique for holding minuscule screws and wires, his three fingers working in a coordinated dance, each movement precise and efficient. He adapted his tools, creating custom-sized wrenches and screwdrivers from scraps of metal and wood, perfectly suited to his hand. He even fashioned a miniature vise from a repurposed clothespin, proving his ingenuity in overcoming constraints.

The miniature rocket engine was particularly challenging. He had initially envisioned using a small, commercially available model rocket engine, but the size was too large for his spacecraft. This setback didn't discourage him. Instead, he meticulously researched the physics of rocket propulsion, learning about thrust, specific impulse, and the principles of combustion. He consulted countless online resources, poring over diagrams and specifications, learning about the science behind different types of rocket engines.

He realized he needed to design and build his own miniature engine. This was a daunting task, requiring knowledge of chemistry, engineering, and precision machining. His grandpa, a retired engineer with a workshop full of tools and a lifetime of experience, became an invaluable mentor. Neil spent countless hours in the workshop, learning about materials, tools, and techniques. His grandpa taught him about the importance of precision, safety, and patience. He learned to use a lathe to turn small pieces of metal and wood. He learned to use a drill press to create precise holes. And he learned to use a soldering iron to connect electrical components.

Grandpa didn't just offer instruction; he provided encouragement and unwavering support. He recognized the determination in Neil's eyes, the same spark that had driven him through his own life's challenges. He emphasized the importance of perseverance, reminding Neil that setbacks were inevitable, but that the journey of learning and discovery was just as important as the final result.

The design process was iterative. Neil built several prototypes, each one improved by learning from the failures of earlier attempts. Some rockets exploded prematurely, others sputtered and fizzled, and a few simply refused to ignite. But with each failure, he analyzed what went wrong, refined his designs, and applied his growing knowledge of physics and engineering. He meticulously documented his experiments, noting every detail of his successes and failures. This record helped him trace the development of his skills and track his progress.

Collaboration played a critical role in Neil's success. His friends, initially spectators of his experiments, quickly became active participants. Mark, with his mathematical skills, helped Neil calculate the best propellant mix and nozzle size. Kevin, with his artistic flair, designed aesthetically pleasing and aerodynamically sound fins for the rocket. Jason, adept at electronics, helped with the design and construction of the launch control system. This collaboration created a dynamic exchange of ideas and problem-solving techniques.

Their teamwork extended beyond technical ability. They provided moral support, celebrated Neil's successes, and encouraged him during setbacks. They understood his dedication, and they stood by him as he overcame every obstacle. These shared experiences forged deep bonds, building a friendship that would last for years.

The setting for Neil's journey was multifaceted, shifting between the sterile environment of his meticulously organized workshop, the serene atmosphere of the town library, and the warmth and comfort of his home. His workshop was a testament to his dedication, a chaotic yet organized space filled with tools, materials, half-finished projects, and the scent of sawdust and glue. The library, as always, served as a refuge, a place where he could immerse himself in knowledge. And his home provided a sanctuary, a place of rest and reflection, where he could share his triumphs and setbacks with family and friends.

The construction of the rocket engine required a level of precision that even Neil's adapted techniques couldn't fully manage. Some of the components were too small and delicate for his hands. A standard soldering iron produced too much heat for the finer parts. This led him to design a specialized tool using a small heating element and a magnifying glass, allowing him to work with better precision. It was a testament to his ingenuity that he overcame this challenge with a tool of his own creation.

As the launch day approached, a new obstacle appeared: the wind. A strong wind was forecast, threatening to deflect the rocket's trajectory. Neil and his friends brainstormed several solutions, ranging from building a windbreak to designing a more stable launch system. In the end, they developed a three-point launch system, providing extra support and stability against the wind.

The culmination of Neil's efforts was a testament to his resilience and determination. The launch, watched by a small crowd of friends, family, and schoolmates, was a success. The miniature rocket soared into the sky, its flight a symbol of Neil's journey. It wasn't just the launch that mattered; it was the process of learning, problem-solving, and collaboration that had brought him to that moment.

The success wasn't only about a rocket in the sky. It was about his spirit, his creative problem-solving, and the strength he gained from those around him. The journey to overcome each obstacle had been just as important as the final result. It reminded him of his potential and prepared him for the greater challenges ahead. His path toward the stars was clearer now, and this was only the beginning.

CHAPTER 8:

THE POWER OF IMAGINATION

The triumphant launch of his miniature rocket, a testament to his ingenuity and perseverance, left Neil buzzing with excitement. Yet, the feeling was bittersweet. While he had conquered the technical challenges, a nagging sense of incompleteness lingered. He'd built and launched a rocket, but he hadn't actually experienced space travel. The yearning to feel the weightlessness, to see the curvature of the Earth from above, remained a powerful pull.

This yearning lit up a fresh idea. He couldn't physically travel to space, but he could imagine being there. He could share that imagination with his friends. The idea blossomed in his mind: he would create a virtual reality experience, a simulated space journey, using nothing but cardboard, paint, and his boundless imagination.

The project began simply enough. He started with a large cardboard box, the kind that once held a refrigerator. This would be his spaceship's hull. He meticulously measured and cut openings for portholes, using smaller boxes and tubes to fashion control panels, levers, and even a makeshift joystick. He painted the exterior a deep, lustrous black, speckled with silver to mimic the appearance of a spacecraft. Inside, he used vibrant colours like deep blues for the simulated Earth, swirling purples and oranges for nebulae, and twinkling silver stars meticulously glued to the ceiling.

But Neil's ambition didn't stop at mere aesthetics. He wanted to create an immersive experience, a journey that engaged all senses. He used everyday materials in creative ways. Empty soda bottles, filled with varying amounts of water, became gravity simulators. He used a fan to create the sensation of wind rushing past the spacecraft during simulated atmospheric re-entry. He even fashioned a rudimentary rumble effect by placing a small motor under the pilot's seat (an upturned bucket), allowing for subtle vibrations that felt like rocket thrust.

The portholes were particularly impressive. He meticulously cut circular openings and inserted clear plastic sheets onto which he painstakingly painted breathtaking landscapes. One showed a swirling, vibrant nebula, its colours so vivid they seemed to pulse with light. Another depicted the Earth, a breathtaking blue marble suspended in the inky blackness of space. He even created a simulated lunar landscape, complete with craters and the desolate beauty of the moon's surface.

He worked tirelessly, often spending hours lost in his creative world. The process was therapeutic, a way of escaping the limitations of his physical reality and immersing himself in a realm where imagination reigned supreme. His work was driven not by a need for perfection, but by a deep-seated passion for space exploration and a desire to share that passion with others.

As his virtual reality spaceship took shape, Neil involved his friends. Mark, with his sharp eye for detail, helped with the precise painting of the constellations. Kevin, always the artist, designed and painted compelling scenes for the portholes. Jason, ever the technician, helped wire the small motor for the rumble effect and perfect the airflow from the fan. The collaboration was as much about creative brainstorming and artistic design as it was about the technical aspects of the project. Their shared passion and teamwork fueled the project's momentum.

The finished product was nothing short of remarkable. The spaceship, a testament to their shared ingenuity, was an impressive structure, a vibrant blend of artistry and engineering. The interior was a captivating space, rich in detail and alive with imagination.

The attention to detail was exquisite, from the perfectly scaled control panels to the realistically painted planetary landscapes visible through the portholes.

The unveiling of Neil's creation was met with awe and wonder. His friends were captivated by the immersive experience. They climbed inside, took turns at the makeshift joystick, and marveled at the vibrant landscapes, feeling the gentle vibrations of the "thrusters" and the cooling breeze from the simulated atmospheric re-entry.

They spent hours exploring the virtual universe that Neil had so painstakingly created. Laughter filled the air as they shared the experience, exploring the imagined cosmos together.

The success of the virtual reality spaceship wasn't just about creating a fun game or an engaging project. It was about proving how far imagination could go and how creativity could overcome physical limitations. Neil's project served as a beacon of inspiration for his friends, showing them that their limitations were only bound by the limits of their own imaginations. It was a touching reminder that ingenuity, resourcefulness, and collaborative spirit could transform even the most challenging of circumstances into opportunities for creativity and joy.

The project also had a profound impact on Neil himself. The act of creation was deeply satisfying, a powerful affirmation of his capabilities. He discovered new strengths and skills, furthering his understanding of design, engineering, and collaborative problem-solving. The experience wasn't just about building a spaceship; it was about building confidence, resilience, and belief in his own abilities.

Neil's journey wasn't just about the creation of a fantastic cardboard spaceship. It was about conquering limitations, fostering friendships, and discovering the unlimited potential within himself. It was a testament to the extraordinary power of the human spirit, the capacity for innovation, and the unwavering strength that comes from believing in oneself. His virtual reality spaceship, a product of his creativity and perseverance, was a metaphor for his own incredible journey towards fulfilling his dreams, a journey that, despite challenges, continued its trajectory towards the stars. The experience cemented a strong belief in him: that his journey to space, while physically challenging, was always attainable in the boundless realm of his imagination. He realized that the true exploration wasn't confined to the physical universe; it existed in the limitless expanse of his creativity. This understanding gave him the fuel to pursue his dreams, one creative leap at a time. The journey to space might be long, but with each project, each imaginative leap, he was getting closer.

CHAPTER 9:

A NEW PERSPECTIVE

The resounding success of his virtual reality spaceship project filled Neil with a newfound sense of purpose. He'd proven to himself, and to his friends, that his unique perspective and three-fingered hand were not limitations, but rather strengths that helped him tackle problems in creative and innovative ways. This realization sparked a new avenue of exploration – a deeper dive into the history of space exploration itself. He wanted to learn about the scientists, engineers, and astronauts who had paved the way, those who had overcome obstacles, defied expectations, and reached for the stars.

His research began in the dusty attic of his grandfather's house, a treasure trove of old books and forgotten magazines. He unearthed a collection of biographies, scientific journals, and even vintage National Geographic magazines, each page filled with captivating stories of human ingenuity and perseverance. He spent hours flipping through these chronicles, his fingers tracing the faded photographs of groundbreaking scientists and daring astronauts.

One name that particularly captivated him was that of Dr. Katherine Johnson, a brilliant mathematician whose calculations were instrumental in the success of early NASA missions. Neil was mesmerized by her story, how she overcame racial segregation and gender discrimination to achieve remarkable feats in a field dominated by men. He learned about her unwavering dedication to accuracy, her meticulous attention to detail, and her unwavering belief in the power of mathematics. Her story resonated deeply with Neil; it showed him that obstacles, no matter how significant, could be overcome with sheer determination and a refusal to compromise on excellence.

He then delved into the life of Valentina Tereshkova, the first woman to travel to space. Tereshkova's journey was a testament to courage, resilience, and the breaking of barriers. Neil was deeply moved by her story, her fearless chase of a dream despite the significant challenges she faced as a woman in a male-dominated field. Her perseverance inspired him to pursue his own dreams with even greater determination. It was a powerful reminder that limitations are often self-imposed and that with enough courage and conviction, anything is possible.

His research extended beyond the pioneers of space travel. He learned about Stephen Hawking, a theoretical physicist who made groundbreaking contributions to our understanding of the universe despite battling a debilitating disease. Hawking's life was a testament to the indomitable human spirit, a demonstration that intellectual curiosity and the pursuit of knowledge could transcend physical limitations. Neil admired Hawking's relentless pursuit of understanding, his ability to communicate complex ideas with clarity and passion, and his inspirational message that nothing was out of reach if you refused to give up.

The more Neil researched, the more he realized that the history of space exploration was not just a story of technological advancement, but also a story of human resilience, ingenuity, and the overcoming of adversity. He found himself drawn to the stories of individuals who had faced significant challenges—individuals with disabilities, from diverse backgrounds, and those who had overcome seemingly insurmountable odds. Their stories provided him with a sense of comfort and affirmation; he wasn't alone in his struggles.

He discovered the remarkable contributions of scientists and engineers who had approached challenges with unique perspectives and innovative solutions. He learned about scientists who used unconventional methods to achieve breakthroughs, engineers who designed ingenious solutions with limited resources, and astronauts who displayed exceptional courage and adaptability in the face of unexpected circumstances. Again and again, it became clear to Neil that the most groundbreaking ideas often came from people who saw things differently.

Neil began to see his own "difference" – his shorter arm and three-fingered hand – not as a deficiency but as a unique perspective. He realized that his way of problem-solving, honed through years of adapting to his physical condition, could potentially be a valuable asset in the field of space exploration. He started to think about how his unique approach might allow him to design more efficient and innovative tools or to find creative solutions to engineering challenges.

His research also helped him develop a deeper understanding of the scientific principles underlying space travel. He devoured books on astronomy, astrophysics, and rocket science, gaining a profound appreciation for the complexity and wonder of the universe. He learned about the forces of gravity, the dynamics of orbital mechanics, and the challenges of interplanetary travel. This knowledge not only fueled his passion for space exploration but also provided him with the technical background needed to further develop his own creative projects.

Inspired by the stories of those who had come before him, Neil began to see the path ahead with renewed clarity. He realized that his journey to space wouldn't be a simple one; it would require dedication, perseverance, and a willingness to overcome challenges. He also understood that his unique perspective, his inventive spirit, and his unwavering determination could make his dream a reality.

The next step in his journey was to build a more sophisticated model rocket, incorporating the knowledge he had gained from his research. This time, he wasn't just focused on the aesthetic appeal; he wanted to create a functional model that incorporated advanced principles of rocket propulsion and flight dynamics. He meticulously researched different types of rocket engines, studying their designs and the principles behind their operation. He spent weeks poring over technical diagrams, calculations, and experiments, meticulously documenting every step of his research and development process.

He used his newfound knowledge of aerodynamics to design a more streamlined rocket body, minimizing air resistance and maximizing efficiency. He experimented with different materials, striving to achieve the best balance between weight and strength. He even explored the possibility of using alternative fuels, researching the properties of different propellants and their potential for increased performance.

The design process was challenging, requiring meticulous planning, countless calculations, and a significant amount of patience. But Neil's persistence, coupled with his growing understanding of rocket science, proved to be invaluable. His three-fingered hand, once a source of frustration, became a tool of precision, enabling him to assemble delicate components and perform intricate tasks with exceptional dexterity.

The construction of this new rocket became a personal journey of growth and self-discovery, a testament to his resilience, ingenuity, and unwavering belief in himself. The process was not always easy, filled with setbacks and moments of doubt, but Neil persevered, driven by an unyielding passion and a determination to succeed. The many failed attempts only served to strengthen his resolve and refine his understanding of the complex principles governing rocket propulsion and flight.

His new rocket, a significant improvement over his earlier model, was a testament to his hard work, dedication, and relentless pursuit of knowledge. The meticulous design, the carefully selected materials, and the precise construction reflected his growing understanding of rocket science and engineering. It was a symbol of his unwavering determination to overcome the physical limitations that once seemed insurmountable.

The successful launch of his second rocket was more than just a technical achievement. It was a culmination of his journey of self-discovery, a powerful affirmation of his abilities, and a profound statement about the power of perseverance. The rocket soared into the sky, a beacon of hope and a symbol of his unwavering determination to reach for the stars. The feeling was different this time; it wasn't just bittersweet. This launch was filled with a deep sense of accomplishment and a profound understanding that the path to fulfilling his dream was not only possible but well within his reach. It solidified his belief that his unique perspective, rather than hindering him, was an asset, giving him a powerful edge in problem-solving and innovation. His journey to space was no longer just a dream; it was a tangible goal, fueled by knowledge, perseverance, and a deep-seated belief in the power of his own potential.

35

CHAPTER 10:

SHARING HIS PASSION

The successful launch of his improved model rocket wasn't just a personal victory; it sparked a ripple effect within his family. His younger siblings, eight-year-old Lily and six-year-old Tom, had been eager observers throughout his entire project. They'd seen his dedication, his struggles, and ultimately, his hard-earned success. Their wide-eyed wonder as the rocket soared into the sky mirrored Neil's own awe and excitement, but with an added layer of pure admiration for their older brother.

Lily, ever the inquisitive one, bombarded Neil with questions after the launch. "How did you make it go so high, Neil?" she asked, her eyes sparkling with fascination. "Did you use magic?"

Neil chuckled, enjoying the opportunity to share his passion. "No magic, Lily," he replied, patiently explaining the principles of rocket propulsion in words she could understand. He used simple analogies, comparing the thrust of the rocket engine to a powerful balloon releasing air, and the trajectory to the arc of a bouncing ball.

Tom, though younger, was equally enthralled. He wasn't interested in the technical details as much as he was in the sheer spectacle of the rocket's flight. He mimicked the rocket's ascent, arms outstretched, making whooshing noises and pretending to steer an imaginary spacecraft.

This playful imitation highlighted the infectious nature of Neil's enthusiasm.

Neil decided to use this newfound fascination, transforming his basement into a makeshift space exploration center. He set up his laptop, projecting the immersive virtual reality spaceship experience he'd created onto a large screen. Lily and Tom, initially hesitant, soon found themselves completely engrossed in the simulation. They navigated the virtual spaceship with Neil's guidance, exploring the vastness of space and marveling at the simulated planets and stars.

Neil narrated their journey, weaving tales of astronauts, planets, and galaxies, bringing to life the stories he'd unearthed in his research. He explained the challenges faced by real astronauts, the scientific principles behind space travel, and the wonders of the universe, all tailored to their level of understanding. He showed them images of nebulae, pulsars, and distant galaxies, sparking their imaginations with the sheer scale and beauty of the cosmos.

Lily, ever the adventurer, took the controls of the virtual spaceship, navigating through asteroid fields and docking at a simulated space station. Tom, playing the role of a space engineer, offered suggestions on course correction and equipment operation, mirroring the collaborative spirit he had seen in Neil's work. Their laughter filled the basement as they maneuvered the virtual spacecraft through the cosmos.

Neil's passion proved contagious. He didn't just teach them about space; he taught them about perseverance, problem-solving, and the power of pursuing their dreams, no matter how ambitious. He explained how his three-fingered hand, initially perceived as a limitation, had become an asset, shaping his unique approach to problem-solving. He emphasized that every individual has unique strengths and perspectives, and that these differences should be celebrated, not treated as deficiencies.

The virtual space exploration sessions became a regular occurrence, transforming their basement into a hub of learning and imaginative play. Neil designed interactive games and activities related to space exploration, incorporating puzzles, quizzes, and creative challenges that fostered their critical thinking and problem-solving skills.

One evening, Neil decided to share his physical model of the spaceship with Lily and Tom. He explained the intricacies of its design, pointing out the features that were inspired by real spacecraft, and the ones he had designed himself. He allowed them to examine the model closely, explaining the different parts and their functions. They were captivated by the craftsmanship and ingenuity displayed in the model. Tom especially loved the intricate details of the model rockets' boosters, fascinated by the mechanics of how it launched. Lily, intrigued by Neil's attention to detail, noticed the small imperfections, appreciating the handmade effort behind it. It became clear to Neil that his younger siblings, while captivated by the spectacle, were also learning to appreciate the creativity, ingenuity, and effort behind his creation.

He showed them pictures and videos from his research, showcasing the diverse group of people who have contributed to space exploration throughout history. He shared stories of people from various backgrounds and with differing abilities, all united by their passion for space. He explained how these individuals had overcome obstacles and challenges to achieve extraordinary feats, emphasizing the importance of diversity and inclusion in the field of science and technology.

Inspired by Neil's tales, Lily decided she wanted to become an astronaut. She announced her ambition with the same unwavering confidence that Neil had shown during his own journey. Tom, on the other hand, expressed interest in becoming a rocket scientist, eagerly asking Neil about the technical aspects of the space program and his own creations. The impact of Neil's sharing his passion reached even deeper than he had imagined.

Neil's influence extended beyond his siblings. Word of his virtual reality spaceship and his remarkable model rockets spread throughout his school. Other children, inspired by his tenacity and success, started expressing interest in STEM subjects. Neil, feeling a responsibility for this newfound influence, decided to organize a presentation for his class, showcasing his work and sharing his passion. He showed the virtual reality experience, providing his classmates with an opportunity to immerse themselves in the wonders of space. He brought his model rockets, explaining the principles of design and propulsion in an engaging way, encouraging their curiosity and exploration.

His presentation was a huge success. His classmates were captivated by his enthusiasm, his insightful explanations, and his story of overcoming his limitations. Several students approached him afterward, expressing interest in learning more about space exploration and seeking his guidance on their own projects. Neil's inspiring journey had ignited a spark of enthusiasm, encouraging his peers to explore their own passions and dreams. The success of his presentation confirmed the contagious nature of his passion, and he realized the responsibility that came with sharing his inspiration. His journey to space was now not just a personal pursuit but also a mission to inspire others. He started to see his unique perspective as a way to connect with people, especially those who felt like outsiders.

That night, after a fulfilling day of sharing his passion, Neil sat in his room, gazing at the night sky. The stars, once distant objects of fascination, now felt a little bit closer. He was no longer just dreaming of space; he was actively building a bridge to it, inviting others to dream alongside him. His own journey had changed its trajectory; it was no longer merely about reaching for the stars, but also about bringing the wonder of the stars to others. His three-fingered hand, his shorter arm, the limitations that defined his childhood, now felt like badges of honor, symbols of spirit, and testament to his unwavering passion. He knew his journey to space would be challenging, but he was ready, emboldened by the fact that he wasn't alone in his aspirations. He was leading a small, enthusiastic fleet of young dreamers, each one inspired by his unique story and unwavering belief in the power of dreams. He realized that this was a journey, sharing what he loved and lifting others up, was even more fulfilling than the one to space itself. The universe, it seemed, held endless possibilities, not only for his own journey, but for the many young minds he now had the privilege of inspiring.

CHAPTER 11:

THE SCHOOL SCIENCE FAIR

The school science fair loomed large on the horizon, a vibrant tapestry woven with anticipation and a healthy dose of nervous energy. Neil, armed with his meticulously crafted spaceship model, felt a familiar flutter of excitement mixed with a touch of anxiety. This wasn't just another project; it was the result of months of dedicated work, a testament to his unwavering passion, and a chance to share his dream with a wider audience. He had poured his heart and soul into the model, incorporating elements assembled from countless hours of research, carefully recreating intricate details, and devising innovative solutions to challenges presented by his physical limitations.

His three-fingered hand, once a source of insecurity, had become his greatest ally, shaping his unique approach to design and problem-solving. He had learned to adapt, to find creative workarounds, and in doing so, had developed a skill set as unique as his fingerprint. His shorter arm, once seen as an obstacle, had only pushed him harder to prove that limitations are often just beliefs, easily overcome with creativity and determination.

The day of the science fair dawned bright and clear, the sun casting a warm glow on the bustling school gymnasium.

Tables were meticulously arranged, each showcasing a student's project, a testament to their ingenuity and creativity. The air buzzed with energy: a mix of excited chatter, the whirring of motors, and the occasional gasp of awe. Neil found his assigned space and carefully placed his spaceship model in the center of the display, surrounded by his crafted informational panels, complete with diagrams, schematics, and detailed descriptions of his design process.

He had carefully planned every aspect of his presentation, aiming for a mix of technical accuracy and engaging storytelling. He wanted to share not just the technical details of the spaceship but the personal journey behind it. He hoped to inspire others not only through the finished project, but by showing the determination and resilience that had gone into it.

As the judges began their rounds, Neil felt a surge of nervous energy. He had expected tough questions and had prepared detailed answers to demonstrate his understanding of the scientific principles behind his work. He confidently explained the aerodynamics of his rocket, the complexities of his navigation system, and the clever solutions he had used to address structural challenges. He walked the judges through his design choices with clarity and passion, showing how his unique perspective had shaped his way of thinking.

The judges, a mix of science teachers, local engineers, and university professors, were impressed by the sophistication of his design, the precision in his craftsmanship, and the way he explained it all. They were especially struck by Neil's ability to adapt to his physical challenges and turn them into advantages. His project reflected perseverance, ingenuity, and a deep love for space exploration.

His presentation didn't just show his technical abilities; it revealed his strength as a storyteller. He spoke about his grandpa's encouragement, the long hours spent researching and building, and the moments when he felt like giving up. He talked about how facing challenges head-on had helped him grow, inspiring the judges with his ability to turn obstacles into opportunities.

The competition was tough. Other students brought impressive work: robots with advanced sensors, complex code-based projects, and experiments that revealed sharp scientific thinking. But Neil's project stood out for its blend of creativity and engineering, backed by a personal story. His model wasn't just a display piece, it was a dream made real, a symbol of his drive, and proof that believing in yourself can take you far.

When it was time for the winners to be announced, the room filled with excited energy. Every name called brought cheers, some sighs, and a lot of suspense. When Neil's name was announced as one of the winners, a wave of happiness washed over him. All his effort, all the setbacks, and long nights had all been worth it.

The prize ceremony felt like a moment he'd remember forever. Neil, smiling proudly, accepted his award, not just for the recognition, but for the journey it represented. His younger siblings, Lily and Tom, cheered loudly from the audience, their faces lit up with excitement and pride.

What happened next surprised him. News of his project and his story started spreading. A local newspaper ran a feature about him; how he used creativity to solve problems, how he turned challenges into strengths, and how his passion for space had carried him through. The article resonated with readers. People were inspired.

But for Neil, the science fair wasn't just about winning. It was about sharing his dream, helping others feel inspired, and proving that everyone has something valuable to offer. His success gave him confidence, and it gave others hope. Students who had felt like they didn't belong suddenly saw themselves in Neil. He showed them that being different doesn't mean being less, and that chasing your dream is always worth it.

In the weeks that followed, Neil's model became more than just a project. It became a source of encouragement to others. His creative approach and belief in himself helped classmates push past their own doubts. The fair wasn't just a contest anymore, it had become a spark for something bigger. More students began showing interest in STEM subjects. Neil's journey had lit a path others now wanted to follow.

His spaceship, built with care, resilience, and heart, became a symbol. It stood for the idea that big dreams start with small steps. The stars, once so far away, now seemed closer than ever. And Neil, with his three-fingered hand, his shorter arm, and a head full of ideas, was ready to reach for them.

Chapter 12:

Unexpected Friendship

The hum of excited chatter filled the gymnasium, a vibrant tapestry woven with the energy of aspiring young scientists. Neil, still basking in the afterglow of his science fair victory, carefully adjusted a loose wire on his spaceship model. He felt a lightness in his step, a newfound confidence that hadn't been there before. The win wasn't just about the trophy; it was proof that his dream mattered, a testament to his perseverance in the face of his physical differences.

As he straightened up, a girl with bright, inquisitive eyes approached his display. She had a cascade of dark brown hair that framed her face, lit up with curiosity. Her eyes, the color of warm honey, were fixed on his meticulously crafted spaceship, tracing the intricate details with her gaze.

"Wow," she breathed, her voice soft yet filled with genuine admiration. "This is incredible. It's... it's awesome!"

Neil, slightly taken aback by her enthusiasm, managed a shy smile. "Thanks," he said, his face turning red.

"I'm Maya," she introduced herself, extending a hand. Her grip was firm, her smile immediately disarming.

"Neil," he replied, shaking her hand. Her touch was surprisingly reassuring, a comforting warmth that eased his usual shyness.

Maya spent the next few minutes examining his spaceship, asking insightful questions about its design and functionality. She didn't just focus on the technical stuff; she was curious about the story behind it too. She asked about his journey, his struggles, and what kept him going. She listened carefully as he explained the challenges he'd faced, his innovative fixes, and the huge role his grandfather had played in supporting him. He found himself opening up to her in a way he hadn't with anyone else before.

Her questions weren't just casual; they dug deep, showing she understood and cared. She asked about the aerodynamics of his rocket, the details of his navigation system, and the materials he had used, clearly knowing a thing or two about aerospace herself. She even pointed out a small feature in his model that he hadn't noticed before, which led to a fun back-and-forth about how he might improve it.

As they talked, Neil realized they shared the same spark when it came to space. Maya, it turned out, was just as obsessed with the stars. She talked about her own science projects, her love for astrophysics, and how she wanted to be an astronaut one day. Her energy was contagious, making Neil feel even more excited about his own goals.

They jumped from topic to topic, from the latest discoveries in exoplanet research to the crazy challenges of traveling between stars. The conversation just kept flowing, full of ideas, jokes, and big dreams. They debated the pros and cons of different propulsion methods, argued playfully about colonizing Mars versus Europa, and imagined what life might look like on alien worlds.

Around them, other students stayed busy with their own displays, but Neil barely noticed. Talking to Maya felt like being in their own little world, a space filled with encouragement and understanding. They ended up chatting for hours, long after the science fair was supposed to wind down.

Neil found himself drawn not just to her knowledge, but to the way she saw him. She didn't act like his challenges defined him. She saw his creativity, his persistence, and how he solved problems in his own way. Unlike people who only saw what he couldn't do, Maya focused on what he could.

As the day came to an end and the fair began to wrap up, there was a warm buzz in the air. Students congratulated each other, swapped ideas, and laughed together. What started as a competition now felt more like a team effort.

Neil and Maya exchanged contact info, promising to work on something together soon. Their friendship, sparked by a shared love for space, already felt like something special. It was a connection built on common dreams and the rare feeling of really being seen by someone else.

In the days that followed, Neil felt recharged. He wasn't chasing his goals alone anymore, he had Maya. They kicked off their collaboration with long video calls, bouncing ideas around and laughing over their different approaches.

They brainstormed projects, from building a more advanced rocket using Maya's physics knowledge to creating an outreach program to get more kids excited about science. Maya brought solid theory. Neil brought big ideas and design skills. Together, they made a great team. Their projects weren't just technical; they were fun, creative, and full of back-and-forth brainstorming that pushed both of them further.

Soon, they started preparing a presentation for a regional science and tech fair. They split the work based on what each of them did best, and found that their differences made their work stronger. Neil's out-of-the-box thinking was grounded by Maya's precision. Their presentation wasn't just smart—it had heart. They talked about their experiences, their teamwork, and how they supported each other through every challenge.

Their message really hit home. The judges and audience were moved, not just by the science, but by the story. They showed how two very different people could come together to make something amazing. The presentation sparked conversations about teamwork, inclusion, and the value of different perspectives.

The recognition they got wasn't just about the project. Their story ended up in local and national news. Young people everywhere, especially those who felt like they didn't fit in, saw themselves in Neil and Maya. Their friendship, built on mutual respect and a shared dream, became a symbol of what's possible when you stop worrying about fitting in and start focusing on what really matters.

Neil and Maya's unlikely friendship had

become something bigger than they expected. It stood for hope, for creativity, and for the amazing things that can happen when you believe in yourself and find someone who believes in you too. Their journey was just beginning. And now, with each new step, space didn't feel like a far-off fantasy anymore, it felt possible.

The sky, once unreachable, was now a destination within sight, made clearer and closer by friendship, passion, and a belief in what could be.

CHAPTER 13:

FACING CRITICISM

The regional science and technology fair was a whirlwind of activity. The air crackled with anticipation, a palpable energy that thrummed through the brightly lit exhibition hall. Neil and Maya, surrounded by their meticulously crafted display, felt a familiar blend of excitement and nerves. Their presentation, a testament to their collaborative efforts and shared passion, stood as a beacon of innovation and inclusivity. They had poured their hearts and souls into it, weaving together their individual strengths into a cohesive narrative that resonated with their shared dream: reaching for the stars.

However, amidst the celebratory atmosphere, a shadow loomed. During a break between presentations, a group of adults, teachers, and school administrators, gathered near their display, their conversation low but distinctly critical. Neil overheard snippets of their discussion, words like "unrealistic," "naive," and "beyond his capabilities" piercing his carefully constructed bubble of confidence.

Their comments focused not on the technical brilliance of their project but on Neil's physical difference, suggesting that his achievements were somehow less significant because of it.

The sting of their words was sharp, unexpectedly so. The validation he had received from Maya and the judges seemed to fade into the background, replaced by a familiar wave of self-doubt. He felt the ache of inadequacy, the insidious whisper that his dreams were nothing more than childish fantasies, fueled by an unrealistic optimism. He glanced at Maya, her expression unreadable. She hadn't heard the comments but could sense something had shifted.

He tried to dismiss their words, to brush them off as the opinions of people who didn't understand his passion.

Unfortunately, the seed of doubt had been planted, taking root in his confidence. He found himself retreating inside himself, his usual enthusiasm waning. The vibrant energy he'd previously exuded seemed to dim, replaced by a hesitant uncertainty.

Maya, sensing his discomfort, gently placed a hand on his arm. Her touch, a familiar comfort, grounded him in the present. "What's wrong?" she asked, her voice a soft balm to his troubled spirit.

He hesitated, unsure how to explain what he'd heard. He tried to articulate it, stammering slightly, his voice barely above a whisper. He told her about the criticism, the doubts they had sown, and the sting of feeling underestimated because of his physical difference.

Maya listened closely, her eyes filled with understanding. When he finished, she squeezed his arm, her expression firm. "Their opinion doesn't matter," she said, her voice strong and steady. "Your work speaks for itself. It's brilliant, and your ability to overcome challenges is even more impressive."

Her words were a lifeline, pulling him back from the edge of discouragement. She didn't brush aside his feelings but acknowledged his hurt and reminded him how far he'd come.

Then she had an idea. She suggested they invite the teachers and administrators back to their booth to ask questions, see the project in detail, and witness Neil's knowledge firsthand. It was a chance to prove them wrong but more than that, a chance to reclaim his confidence.

At first, Neil was unsure. But the more he thought about it, the more he felt ready. It wasn't just about the criticism. It was about reminding himself what he was capable of.

They approached the adults with calm determination, inviting them to return and ask any questions they liked. The group, slightly surprised, agreed with curious expressions.

Neil and Maya led them through the project, answering questions clearly and confidently. Neil explained the complex engineering principles behind the design, offering detailed, thoughtful responses. He didn't shy away from the technical aspects; he embraced them, walking through each element with ease and purpose.

As he spoke, his nervousness faded. In its place came a quiet confidence. He explained how his physical difference had led him to think creatively, solving problems in ways others hadn't considered. His three-fingered hand, once a source of insecurity, now moved with precision as he pointed to diagrams and demonstrated model components.

Maya supported him effortlessly, explaining the astrophysical concepts and highlighting how their teamwork had strengthened the project. She emphasized how Neil's input had inspired her own thinking and how his design ideas had pushed them both to work smarter.

Together, they told a story not just of science, but of growth. Of believing in yourself, of learning from setbacks, and of trusting the strength in your differences.

By the end of the conversation, the adults' skepticism had shifted. Their tone softened, their praise genuine. They acknowledged the impact of Neil's work and the depth of his understanding. What had started as quiet doubt ended in clear respect.

For Neil, this moment mattered. Not just because of them, but because of what it meant for him. He had faced the criticism, felt the sting, and pushed through it. He'd proven, to himself most of all, that limitations didn't define him, his persistence and imagination did.

The experience brought him and Maya even closer. Their collaboration, once just an exciting opportunity, now felt like a powerful partnership grounded in mutual trust and belief.

Their journey, shaped by challenges and lifted by hope, had become something bigger than either of them expected. The path ahead still held obstacles, but they were ready, together, for whatever came next. Their shared dream of reaching the stars now felt more real than ever.

Chapter 14:

Expanding Horizons

The science fair victory, while exhilarating, was only a stepping stone. The lingering taste of doubt, though significantly diminished, still prompted Neil to seek further validation, a deeper proof of his potential. The praises were wonderful, but Neil's thirst for knowledge burned brighter than ever. He craved a deeper dive into the cosmos, a more profound exploration of the challenges and triumphs of space exploration. His fascination, once confined to model rockets and science fiction novels, now stretched towards the complex equations and intricate engineering of interstellar travel.

Maya, always his steady companion, became his partner in this new phase of their journey. They decided to expand their horizons beyond the limitations of their high school library. The local college, with its sprawling library and access to advanced research databases, became their new haven. The hallowed halls, initially intimidating, soon became familiar territory, filled with the comforting aroma of old books and the quiet hum of focused study.

The college library was a labyrinth of knowledge. Rows upon rows of bookshelves, stretching towards the high ceilings, held untold secrets of the universe. Neil and Maya navigated this academic landscape with a sense of wonder and purpose. They spent hours poring over textbooks on astrophysics, aerospace engineering, and robotics. Neil, particularly fascinated by robotic missions, devoured articles on the Mars rovers, the complexities of space-based engineering, and the challenges of autonomous navigation in the harsh environment of space.

One particularly absorbing afternoon, Neil stumbled upon a fascinating article on the challenges of interstellar travel. The sheer scale of the undertaking, the vast distances, the immense energy requirements, and the potential hazards of deep space filled him with both awe and determination. He learned about the concept of warp drives, the theoretical possibility of faster-than-light travel, and the daunting technological hurdles that needed to be overcome. The sheer complexity didn't deter him; instead, it fueled his passion, pushing him to learn even more.

Maya, focused on the astrophysical aspects of interstellar travel, researched the potential habitability of exoplanets, studying stellar classifications, planetary formation, and the search for extraterrestrial life. She learned about the Kepler mission and the TESS mission, their groundbreaking discoveries of planets orbiting other stars, and the ongoing efforts to characterize these distant worlds. Her findings gave depth to Neil's technical focus, providing a broader context for his explorations into robotic mission design.

They collaborated seamlessly, sharing their discoveries and insights. Neil, with his innate problem-solving skills, often found innovative ways to address the complex challenges of interstellar travel, proposing novel solutions to issues like radiation shielding, long-duration life support systems, and the challenges of autonomous navigation in uncharted space. Maya, with her profound understanding of astrophysics, helped him refine his designs, ensuring their feasibility and alignment with the realities of the cosmos.

Their research extended beyond the library. They looked for opportunities to apply their knowledge practically. They volunteered at the local planetarium, helping with presentations and stargazing events. They even managed to secure permission to use the college's 3D printing lab to create more sophisticated models of their robotic designs, incorporating advanced features and functionalities. The college professors, initially hesitant about involving two high school students in their research, were gradually won over by Neil and Maya's enthusiasm and dedication. Impressed by their curiosity and drive, the professors came to appreciate their insightful questions, meticulous research, and ability to grasp complex concepts with remarkable speed.

One particular professor, Dr. Aris Thorne, an expert in robotics and AI, took a special interest in Neil's work. He recognized the unique perspective Neil brought to problem-solving, his innovative approach to design, and his unwavering determination to overcome challenges. Dr. Thorne saw in Neil not just a gifted student but a young innovator with immense potential. He invited Neil to attend his advanced robotics lectures, granting him access to innovative research and fostering his passion for space exploration.

These lectures exposed Neil to new frontiers of robotic technology, including artificial intelligence, machine learning, and swarm robotics. He learned about the development of advanced sensors, actuators, and communication systems crucial for successful space missions. He took part in discussions, debated complex concepts, and shared his own creative ideas, often surprising the other students with his insights.

The college environment, initially daunting, transformed into a nurturing ground for Neil's aspirations. He found himself surrounded by like-minded individuals, students and professors who shared his passion for space exploration and encouraged his unconventional approach to problem-solving. He learned that his unique perspective, once a source of insecurity, was actually a valuable asset, giving him the ability to tackle problems from unexpected angles and find innovative solutions.

One evening, after a particularly insightful lecture on autonomous navigation, Neil and Maya sat in the library, reviewing their notes. They discussed the challenges of interstellar travel, the technological hurdles that stood in their way, and the daunting scale of the task. They were aware of the immense challenges, the potential setbacks, and the long road ahead. Yet, despite the complexities, they felt a renewed sense of purpose, a shared vision that propelled them forward.

The library, once just a repository of knowledge, had become a launching pad for their dreams. The quiet hum of the fluorescent lights seemed to echo with the hum of distant galaxies. The scent of old books blended with the exhilarating air of possibility. Neil and Maya looked at each other, a shared understanding passing between them. The journey to the stars was long, arduous, and fraught with challenges. But they were ready. The path ahead, while uncertain, was illuminated by the light of their unwavering dedication, their shared passion, and their unyielding belief in the power of their dreams. Their journey had expanded beyond the science fair, beyond the high school library, into the vast expanse of human knowledge and innovation. Their limitations had never truly defined them, and their future, bathed in the light of the stars, was boundless. The universe awaited, and they were ready to explore.

CHAPTER 15:

A NEW CHALLENGE

The exhilaration of the science fair victory began to fade, replaced by a steady pulse of ambition. Neil found himself restless, his mind buzzing with ideas far beyond the scope of his earlier model rockets. The intricate designs, once satisfying, now seemed overly basic, childish even. He yearned for a challenge that pushed him beyond his current capabilities, a project that would truly test the limits of his ingenuity and resourcefulness. He wanted to build something... bigger. Something more ambitious.

Something that truly reflected his unwavering dream of space travel.

This new ambition manifested as a vision: a meticulously detailed model of a spacecraft unlike any he'd attempted before. It wouldn't be just a static display; it would be a miniature marvel of engineering, incorporating innovative technological concepts he'd learned about at the college library. He envisioned a vessel equipped with miniature solar panels, a functional robotic arm, and even a rudimentary navigation system. The sheer complexity of the project both daunted and thrilled him. This wasn't just about building a model; it was about pushing the boundaries of what he thought he could achieve.

The initial design phase was a whirlwind of sketches, calculations, and late-night brainstorming sessions with Maya. They spent hours poring over blueprints, technical manuals, and research papers, translating complex aerospace engineering concepts into a format applicable to their miniature spaceship. Neil, with his innate ability to visualize and solve problems, tackled the structural design, meticulously crafting the hull, configuring the propulsion system, and carefully calculating the weight distribution. Maya, his ever-reliable partner, focused on the electrical and mechanical systems, working tirelessly to ensure the functionality of the solar panels, the robotic arm, and the navigation system.

Their collaboration wasn't without its challenges. The intricacies of miniaturizing complex systems presented numerous hurdles. They encountered unexpected problems with the scalability of components, the limitations of the 3D printing process, and the challenges of integrating various subsystems into a cohesive whole. But every setback fueled their determination, pushing them to explore alternative solutions, to think creatively, and to use their combined knowledge and skills.

One particularly frustrating evening, they were struggling with the design of the robotic arm. The miniature motors they'd initially selected lacked the precision and power needed for the intended functionality. Discouraged but not defeated, they spent hours searching for alternatives, painstakingly comparing specifications, and exploring different mechanical designs. Finally, Neil, inspired by a lecture on biomimicry, suggested using a system inspired by the intricate movements of an octopus's arm. The idea, initially met with skepticism, eventually proved to be a brilliant solution, allowing them to create a remarkably nimble and versatile robotic arm using lightweight, flexible materials.

The construction phase was equally demanding. The meticulous work required patience, precision, and unwavering focus. Neil spent countless hours hunched over his workbench, painstakingly assembling the miniature components, soldering delicate wires, and calibrating the various systems. Maya, equally dedicated, ensured the integrity of the electrical connections, programmed the rudimentary navigation system, and thoroughly tested every aspect of the spaceship's functionality. They celebrated small victories, each successful integration a testament to their perseverance and collaborative spirit.

As the project neared completion, Neil encountered a particularly challenging obstacle. The miniature solar panels, essential for powering the spacecraft, weren't generating enough energy to meet the demands of the robotic arm and navigation system. He spent days reviewing his calculations, examining the efficiency of the panels, and exploring alternative energy sources. Finally, he stumbled upon a solution in a research paper on micro-supercapacitors – a technology that could store significant amounts of energy in a remarkably small package. The discovery was a breakthrough, allowing him to incorporate this advanced technology into his design, solving a critical problem and enhancing the spacecraft's functionality.

The final product was a marvel of miniature engineering. The spaceship, no larger than a shoebox, was a testament to Neil and Maya's ingenuity, their unwavering dedication, and their shared passion for space exploration. It boasted a sleek, aerodynamic design, a fully functional robotic arm, a miniature navigation system, and enough power to work for extended periods. It was far more sophisticated than anything they'd ever created before, a true reflection of their growth and development as aspiring engineers.

The unveiling of their creation at the local science fair proved to be a moment of immense pride and satisfaction. The judges, impressed by the complexity and functionality of the model, lauded Neil and Maya's innovative design and problem-solving skills. Their project garnered significant attention, sparking conversations about the potential of miniaturization and the innovative spirit of young minds.

The victory, however, was secondary to the journey itself. The challenges faced, the obstacles overcome, and the lessons learned along the way were invaluable. The

experience had not only honed Neil's engineering skills but had also profoundly changed his self-perception. He'd pushed beyond his perceived limitations, discovering a depth of talent and resilience he hadn't realized he possessed.

This ambitious project served as a powerful reminder: the journey to achieving one's dreams is often fraught with unexpected challenges, but it is precisely these challenges that shape our capabilities and reveal the depths of our potential. Neil's journey was far from over; this sophisticated spaceship model served as a stepping stone, a testament to his growing confidence and a clear sign of his expanding potential to reach for the stars. The next challenge, however, loomed on the horizon — a challenge that would take him far beyond the confines of his workshop and into the wider world of space exploration. The excitement was palpable; the journey had only just begun. The universe, with its mysteries and wonders, awaited.

CHAPTER 16:

THE DESIGN PROCESS

The initial sketches were scattered bursts of creativity on loose sheets of paper—a tangle of lines, curves, and annotations that somehow coalesced into a preliminary design. He used specialized adaptors, meticulously crafted by his grandfather, to enhance his grip and precision, transforming potential hindrances into clever workarounds. He didn't shy away from the complexity; instead, he embraced it, finding a certain satisfaction in the intricate dance between his ingenuity and the physical constraints he faced.

His design incorporated innovative features born from countless hours spent poring over aerospace engineering texts and scientific journals. He envisioned a miniature spacecraft capable of autonomous navigation, powered by tiny, high-efficiency solar cells and equipped with a sophisticated robotic arm for sample collection and manipulation. The robotic arm, a particularly ambitious part, posed a unique challenge. Its movements needed to be precise, yet adaptable enough to handle delicate tasks in a simulated microgravity environment.

Neil's solution involved a bio-inspired design, a system that mimicked the flexible, multi-directional movements of an octopus's arm. He meticulously researched the octopus's anatomy, studying its musculature and neural control mechanisms. He translated these principles into a miniature mechanical system, using flexible polymers and tiny servo motors that allowed the arm to bend, rotate, and grasp with remarkable agility. This wasn't just about replicating the appearance; Neil focused on replicating its movement and responsiveness, translating biological efficiency into a miniature engineering marvel.

The solar panel system was another area that demanded innovative solutions. Miniaturizing these components without sacrificing efficiency proved incredibly difficult. He encountered setbacks, facing power output limitations and challenges in integrating the panels onto the curved surface of his spacecraft model. But Neil, fueled by unwavering determination, researched alternative energy solutions. He delved into the world of micro-supercapacitors, tiny energy storage devices with the potential to overcome the limitations of traditional miniature solar panels.

His research led him to a breakthrough: a novel configuration using both miniaturized solar panels and micro-supercapacitors. The solar panels would charge the supercapacitors during periods of ample sunlight, and the supercapacitors would act as a power buffer, providing a consistent energy supply even in shadow or during periods of low light intensity. This dual system ensured that the robotic arm and the other critical components of his model spacecraft would never lack power, even in simulated dim lighting or when simulating orbital shadowing.

This innovative solution not only solved a critical problem but also made his model spaceship more robust and versatile.

The creation of the spaceship model was far more than just assembling parts; it was a journey of continual learning and adaptation. Neil documented each stage of his design process, meticulously recording his calculations, experiments, and modifications. His detailed notes and sketches acted as both a roadmap and a testament to his dedication, a visual record of his intellectual journey. He even used voice-to-text software to narrate his process, allowing him to dictate notes and observations even as he worked.

He faced several setbacks during the construction process. The delicate nature of the miniature components required exceptional patience and precision. Sometimes, components would break, connections would malfunction, and unforeseen challenges would arise. However, each setback was met with a renewed determination. He treated every problem as a puzzle, and he relished the challenge of finding innovative solutions. His perseverance and innovative spirit propelled him forward. He learned to adapt his techniques, refine his approach, and explore new problem-solving methods.

Neil's unique perspective, born from navigating a world designed for non-disabled individuals, infused his design process with an unusual creativity. He recognized the limitations of existing technologies and found innovative ways to bypass them. He employed assistive technologies, modified conventional tools, and designed custom fixtures to aid in the intricate assembly process. His approach highlighted the power of adaptation and the importance of tailoring solutions to individual circumstances. He proved that limitations, rather than being barriers, could become opportunities for innovation.

The navigational system, a miniature marvel of technology, posed another significant challenge. Neil meticulously designed and programmed a rudimentary autopilot system, ensuring that the spacecraft could follow a predetermined trajectory. This wasn't just about basic movement; he incorporated sensors and algorithms that allowed the spacecraft to react to simulated obstacles and adjust its course dynamically. He achieved this by using open-source software, modifying existing programs to suit the unique requirements of his miniature spaceship. The learning curve was steep, but Neil persevered, teaching himself programming languages and delving into the complex world of embedded systems.

As the model neared completion, Neil focused on the integration of all systems. He painstakingly tested each part individually, then meticulously tested their interaction to ensure seamless operation. This involved countless hours of troubleshooting, adjusting settings, and refining code. He conducted rigorous testing in a simulated microgravity environment, using carefully calibrated apparatus to mimic the conditions of outer space. This thorough testing ensured that his spaceship model would not only look realistic but also function flawlessly.

The final product was an awe-inspiring testament to his ingenuity. It was a miniature spacecraft unlike anything seen before, a marvel of engineering, a reflection of his unwavering determination, and a testament to the power of believing in oneself. It was more than a model; it was a tangible representation of Neil's dream, a symbol of his resilience, and a powerful affirmation of his capabilities. The project wasn't just about the final product; it was about the journey, the challenges overcome, and the lessons learned along the way. It was a journey that solidified Neil's conviction that nothing is impossible if one approaches challenges with creativity, spirit, and an unwavering belief in oneself. He had not only built a spaceship but had also built his confidence, transforming a perceived limitation into a source of strength and inspiration. The final design surpassed even his initial ambitious vision, showcasing his remarkable adaptability and problem-solving prowess. The path ahead remained challenging yet filled with promise, carrying the excitement of continued exploration and the pursuit of his lifelong dream.

CHAPTER 17:

SEEKING MENTORSHIP

The finished model spaceship sat proudly on his workbench, a small but powerful tribute to weeks of relentless effort. It wasn't just a collection of meticulously crafted parts; it was a reflection of Neil's spirit, a physical manifestation of his determination and unshakable dream. Yet, even with its flawless design and intricate mechanisms, a nagging feeling lingered. He knew he needed more. He'd reached a point where his own knowledge, though vast for his age, was beginning to feel like a ceiling rather than a launchpad. He needed guidance—someone experienced who could sharpen his ideas and help him navigate the challenges ahead.

The idea of seeking mentorship hadn't occurred to Neil until he overheard his grandfather discussing a local aerospace engineer, Dr. Aris Thorne, known for his innovative work in miniature robotics.

Grandpa, ever the encourager, suggested that Neil might benefit from a conversation. The thought was initially daunting. What if Dr. Thorne thought he was just a kid playing with toys? What if his unique approach, born from necessity and ingenuity, was considered unconventional and impractical? Fear wrestled with his drive—a familiar internal battle—but the pull of his ambition was stronger.

Gathering his courage, Neil crafted a letter. It wasn't a formal request; it was a heartfelt message that poured out of him in one steady stream, expressing his passion for space exploration, detailing the challenges and triumphs of building his model spaceship, and outlining his aspirations for the future. He included several photographs of his creation, showcasing the intricate details and innovative features. To make his case even stronger, he added a short video demonstrating the miniature spacecraft's autonomous navigation and robotic arm functionality. He knew visuals would speak louder than words alone.

The waiting period felt interminable. Each day stretched long and slow, filled with a mixture of anticipation and unease. He practiced what he would say, imagining himself in Dr. Thorne's presence, explaining his work, answering questions, staying calm. The preparation wasn't only technical—it was personal. He wanted to convey the passion that fueled his ambition. He rehearsed his story, shaping the narrative to capture the essence of his journey: the frustrations, the breakthroughs, and the quiet but powerful belief in himself that never wavered.

Finally, the reply arrived—an invitation to visit Dr. Thorne's workshop. It wasn't a formal letter. It was a handwritten note, simple and sincere, with a tone that immediately eased Neil's nerves. Dr. Thorne expressed his admiration for Neil's creativity and his eagerness to learn more about the project. That short note was more than an invitation—it was a moment of recognition, proof that Neil's work mattered. His hands shook as he read it again, hardly believing it was real.

The workshop was a marvel of organized chaos. Tools of every size and shape were neatly stored but visibly well-used, surrounding complex machinery, intricate circuit boards, and half-finished inventions. The space buzzed with a quiet energy—the kind born from deep focus and bold experimentation. Dr. Thorne, a tall, lean man with kind eyes and a permanently inquisitive look, greeted Neil with a warm, open smile. He wasn't the stern, lab-coated scientist Neil had imagined. He was approachable, curious, and full of energy that matched Neil's own. Within moments, the fear melted away, replaced by awe and a surge of excitement.

Neil, encouraged by Dr. Thorne's welcoming presence, stepped forward with renewed confidence and presented his model spaceship. He meticulously explained the design process, pointing out the key features and highlighting the innovative solutions he had employed. He demonstrated the robotic arm's functionality, showing how it could grasp and manipulate miniature objects with surprising precision. He proudly described the dual solar-panel/and micro-supercapacitor power system, explaining its efficiency and reliability.

Dr. Thorne listened intently, asking insightful questions that went beyond simple observation. He inquired about Neil's design choices, his problem-solving strategies, and his understanding of the underlying principles. He didn't belittle Neil's work or dismiss his ideas; instead, he engaged in a genuine dialogue, offering constructive criticism and suggesting potential improvements. He commended Neil's use of bio-inspired design principles, particularly the octopus-arm-inspired robotic arm, praising its efficiency and adaptability. He challenged Neil to consider alternative materials and manufacturing techniques that could enhance durability and precision.

The conversation flowed naturally, far exceeding Neil's expectations. He discovered that Dr. Thorne had a similar fascination with space exploration, sparking a shared passion that transcended their age difference. Dr. Thorne shared his own experiences, recounting the challenges he faced in his engineering endeavors, and emphasizing the importance of resilience and perseverance. He discussed the significance of continuous learning, the value of collaboration, and the crucial role of mentors in shaping one's path.

Dr. Thorne wasn't just giving technical advice; he was offering a broader perspective, a deeper understanding of the journey ahead. He pointed out the limitations of Neil's current design, suggesting ways to improve efficiency and functionality, while also acknowledging the incredible creativity and ingenuity that had gone into the creation. He spoke about the challenges of miniaturization, the complexities of aerospace engineering, and the long and arduous road to achieving Neil's ambitious goal.

He offered to mentor Neil, guiding him through the complexities of aerospace engineering and helping him refine his designs. This wasn't a formal arrangement with strict guidelines and deadlines; it was a collaborative partnership fueled by shared passion and mutual respect. Dr. Thorne understood the value of nurturing Neil's unique perspective and fostering his creative approach. He recognized that Neil's innovative solutions, often born out of necessity, could help transform conventional approaches to miniature robotics and spacecraft design.

Dr. Thorne's mentorship extended beyond the technical realm. He encouraged Neil to take part in local science fairs and engineering competitions, providing guidance on presentations and strategy. He helped Neil develop his communication skills, teaching him how to articulate his ideas clearly and persuasively. He even introduced Neil to other engineers and scientists, fostering a network of support and collaboration.

The next weeks were filled with intensive learning. Dr. Thorne helped Neil refine the design of his miniature spacecraft, suggesting modifications to enhance stability, efficiency, and functionality. He introduced Neil to advanced software and simulation tools, allowing him to conduct more sophisticated testing and analysis. He taught Neil about materials science, helping him select stronger, lighter, and more durable components for his spacecraft.

Neil, in turn, challenged Dr. Thorne with his unique perspective, questioning conventional approaches and suggesting unconventional solutions. Dr. Thorne was not only impressed by Neil's ingenuity but also inspired by his tenacity and determination. He recognized that Neil possessed a rare combination of creativity, technical aptitude, and unwavering ambition. He saw in Neil not just a bright young mind but a potential innovator who could reshape the landscape of aerospace technology.

Their collaboration produced a significantly improved model spaceship. The revised design incorporated lighter, more durable materials, enhanced navigation systems, and a more sophisticated robotic arm with improved dexterity and precision. The enhanced power system, incorporating a more efficient solar panel configuration and advanced micro-supercapacitors, ensured greater reliability and extended operational time. Neil's original vision had not only been preserved but significantly enhanced by Dr. Thorne's expertise and guidance.

The journey wasn't without its challenges. There were setbacks, moments of frustration, and times when the task seemed insurmountable. But through it all, Neil's determination remained unwavering, sustained by Dr. Thorne's support and encouragement. Dr. Thorne taught Neil how to approach challenges systematically, breaking down complex problems into smaller, more manageable parts. He emphasized the importance of iterative design, continuous testing, and meticulous documentation. He instilled in Neil the value of learning from mistakes, and the significance of embracing failures as opportunities for growth.

Neil's story became an inspiration within the local community. He presented his refined model spaceship at a local science fair, captivating the judges and audience alike. His presentation, a blend of technical prowess and heartfelt passion, garnered accolades and recognition. His story, a testament to the power of determination, became a beacon of hope for children with disabilities, proving that limitations do not define potential.

The mentorship went beyond technical skills; it was a profound influence on Neil's self-belief and confidence. He realized that seeking help isn't a sign of weakness but a mark of strength and self-awareness. He learned the value of collaboration, realizing that even the most brilliant minds benefit from the support and perspectives of others. The collaboration with Dr. Thorne wasn't just about building a better spaceship; it was about building a stronger, more confident, and more determined Neil. His journey had shown him that his dream was not just achievable, but that the journey itself, filled with challenges, mentors, and the unwavering pursuit of one's passion, was equally rewarding. The space beyond the stars was still a distant dream, but the path to reach it was now clearer, brighter, and full of promise.

CHAPTER 18:

TECHNICAL DIFFICULTIES

The initial euphoria following Dr. Thorne's mentorship quickly faded as Neil delved deeper into the construction of his revised spaceship model. While the improved design promised greater efficiency and functionality, it also presented unforeseen technical hurdles. The miniature components, now smaller and more intricate than before, proved incredibly challenging to manipulate with his three-fingered hand. Tasks that would be simple for someone with fully functional hands, like precise soldering, delicate wiring, and the alignment of minuscule gears, became laborious, painstaking processes.

Frustration mounted as seemingly minor setbacks became major obstacles. A misplaced solder joint could make an entire circuit useless, requiring hours of meticulous rework. Tiny screws, barely visible to the naked eye, would slip from his grasp, disappearing into the labyrinthine recesses of his workbench. The delicate balance needed for assembling the miniature gyroscope proved particularly challenging; even the slightest misalignment rendered the stabilization system ineffective.

Neil's first attempts to overcome these challenges were met with limited success. He tried using various tools, including tweezers, magnifying glasses, and even custom-made jigs, but his limited dexterity continued to impede his progress. He spent countless hours wrestling with the miniature components, his frustration growing with each failed attempt. There were moments when he wanted to give up, when the weight of the technical challenges threatened to crush his spirit.

The determination that had always propelled him forward began to falter. However, Neil's resilience, honed over years of adapting to his physical limitations, soon reasserted itself. He refused to let the technical difficulties derail his dream. He began to think differently, employing a more strategic, methodical approach to the problem. He realized that he couldn't simply replicate the methods used by individuals with fully functional hands; he needed to find innovative solutions that catered to his unique abilities.

His first innovation involved redesigning certain components. Instead of relying on tiny screws that were difficult to manipulate, he developed a system of interlocking parts that could be easily assembled and disassembled without the need for intricate fasteners. This involved meticulous planning, precise measurements, and a thorough understanding of the principles of mechanical engineering. He spent hours studying the properties of various materials, searching for the perfect combination of strength, flexibility, and ease of manipulation.

He also embraced the power of collaboration. While he was determined to overcome these obstacles independently, he realized that seeking help wasn't a sign of weakness but a testament to resourcefulness. He approached Dr. Thorne, not with complaints, but with a well-defined set of challenges and a range of potential solutions he had already devised. Dr. Thorne, rather than giving direct answers, guided Neil through a process of problem-solving, encouraging him to explore different approaches and test his hypotheses.

Together, they explored the use of 3D-printing technology to create customized tools tailored to Neil's specific needs. They designed and printed miniature gripping tools with specialized surfaces that provided an improved grip on the tiny components. They also created custom jigs and fixtures that held the components in place, allowing Neil to work on them with greater precision and stability. This hands-on collaboration not only addressed the immediate hurdles but also broadened Neil's understanding of how tools could be designed to match individual needs.

The development of these customized tools wasn't a straightforward process. Several prototypes were created, tested, and refined before a functional design was achieved. Each iteration involved meticulous adjustments, careful experimentation, and a willingness to learn from mistakes. There were moments of frustration, setbacks, and near-discouragement, but Neil's unwavering resolve pushed him through. He learned that even small victories, each incremental improvement in tool design or assembly technique, were crucial steps on the path to success.

Beyond the physical tools, Neil also refined his mental strategies. He developed a systematic approach to assembly, breaking down complex tasks into smaller, more manageable steps. He meticulously planned each stage in advance, predicting potential problems and devising contingency plans. He developed a habit of regular breaks, avoiding the fatigue that could lead to errors and increase the risk of injury. He also learned to accept imperfection, understanding that some level of error was inevitable, but that through careful planning and execution, the errors could be minimized.

The challenges Neil faced taught him valuable lessons about patience, persistence, and the importance of adaptability. He discovered that true innovation isn't always about grand breakthroughs; it's often about the small, incremental improvements and clever workarounds that allow one to overcome obstacles. His experience underscored the need for meticulous planning, the value of creative problem-solving, and the power of unwavering determination in the face of seemingly insurmountable challenges.

As he meticulously assembled the final components of his spaceship model, a sense of profound satisfaction washed over him. It wasn't merely the completion of a project, but the culmination of a journey of perseverance, ingenuity, and self-discovery. The spaceship, a testament to his unwavering determination, stood as a beacon of hope, a symbol of his triumph over seemingly insurmountable challenges. It was a testament not only to his engineering skills but also to the resilience of the human spirit and the indomitable power of dreams. The journey towards space might still be far off, but Neil, armed with his newly gotten skills, his unwavering spirit, and the support of his mentor, felt more confident and prepared than ever before. The technical difficulties, once formidable obstacles, had ultimately become stepping stones on his journey to the stars. His journey had taught him that the path to achieving one's dream is rarely smooth, but the scars of those battles make the final victory all the sweeter.

The final model was a marvel of miniaturization and ingenuity. The improved design incorporated advanced sensors, a more robust control system, and a vastly improved robotic arm capable of intricate manipulations. The power system, a marvel of miniaturization, incorporated innovative solar cells and ultra-high-density micro-supercapacitors, offering extended operational capability. But the true marvel of this model wasn't just its technical sophistication; it was the story it told of resilience, ingenuity, and the human spirit's ability to overcome seemingly impossible obstacles. It was a testament to Neil's unwavering determination, a determination fueled by his dream and sharpened by the challenges he had overcome. The spaceship stood not only as a symbol of his ambition but as a testament to his character, a character forged in the crucible of adversity, strengthened by the unwavering support of his mentor, and illuminated by the enduring power of his dream.

The journey to space stayed a distant prospect, yet Neil, more confident and determined than ever, felt ready to face whatever challenges lay ahead. The stars, once just a distant dream, now felt a little closer, a little more attainable. His journey had shown him that the path to achieving one's dream is rarely straightforward, often littered with unexpected obstacles, but it is the overcoming of these challenges that truly defines the journey and makes the final destination all the more meaningful.

Chapter 19:

Celebrating Small Victories

The satisfying click of the final part snapping into place was more than the culmination of countless hours of painstaking work; it felt like a symphony of small victories. Neil held his breath, his three-fingered hand carefully maneuvering the miniature gyroscope into its designated slot. The delicate mechanism, once the source of so much earlier frustration, now sat perfectly in place; a quiet triumph that reflected his perseverance and ingenuity. A wave of quiet satisfaction washed over him. This wasn't just about building a spaceship model; it was about proving to himself, once again, that he could overcome challenges that once felt impossible.

He carefully examined his creation, tracing the lines of the intricate circuitry with his finger. Each soldered joint, each meticulously placed wire, represented a small battle won. He remembered the countless times he'd almost given up, the moments of frustration when the tiny screws seemed to disappear just to spite him, slipping from his grasp over and over again. He recalled the hours spent researching, experimenting, and refining his techniques, all fueled by an unyielding belief in his dream.

This improved model wasn't merely an upgraded version of his earlier attempt; it was a symbol of his growth. It was a physical manifestation of his journey, a testament to his unwavering determination and the small, almost imperceptible victories that had paved the way to this moment. He realized that the journey itself mattered more than reaching the finish line, at least for now. Each hurdle overcome, each problem solved, had not only enhanced his skills but also fortified his spirit.

He decided to share this momentous occasion, not just with himself but with those who had supported him along the way. First, he called his Grandpa Joe. The familiar warmth of his grandfather's voice filled the room, a comforting counterpoint to the quiet excitement in Neil's heart. He described the intricate details of the model, the challenges he faced, and the innovative solutions he employed.

Grandpa Joe listened patiently, his voice filled with pride and encouragement. "See, Neil," he said, his voice crackling with affection, "even the smallest victories are worth celebrating. They're stepping stones, my boy, each one bringing you closer to your dream."

Neil then excitedly called his best friend, Maya. He described the intricacies of his spaceship design, explaining how he'd adapted his techniques to work around his physical limitations. Maya, ever supportive, listened with rapt attention, her enthusiasm infectious. She understood the size of his accomplishment—not just the technical aspects, but also the immense personal growth it stood for. "It's amazing, Neil," she exclaimed, her voice bubbling with excitement. "You're basically a real-life space engineer now!" Their conversation was filled with shared laughter and encouragement, a reaffirmation of their enduring friendship.

Next, he carefully packed the model and took it to show his parents. His mother's eyes lit up with a mixture of pride and awe as he explained the engineering marvels and the challenges he'd conquered. His father, a man of few words but immense heart, simply nodded, a rare smile gracing his lips as he admired the level of detail and the ingenuity of the design. The simple gesture of his father's approval spoke volumes. His parents had always encouraged him to follow his dreams, reminding him that his physical differences didn't define his potential. Their unwavering support remained a constant source of strength and motivation.

Neil realized that sharing his accomplishments, both big and small, wasn't just about boasting; it was about reinforcing the supportive network that surrounded him.

Sharing his journey with others created a positive feedback loop; it strengthened his resolve and helped keep a positive outlook even when things got tough. The act of celebrating small victories, of acknowledging his progress, helped him stay focused and motivated.

The celebratory mood wasn't confined to phone calls and family gatherings. Neil documented his journey meticulously, creating a detailed record of his design process, the challenges he faced, and the solutions he devised. He snapped clear photos of each step in the process, from the initial sketches and design plans to the final assembly, creating a visual timeline of his progress. He even created short videos, showcasing the intricate details of his work, accompanied by a lighthearted narrative about the ups and downs of the project.

He shared this digital record with his online community, connecting with other space enthusiasts and individuals with similar challenges. He was pleasantly surprised by the overwhelming support and encouragement he received. His story, his struggles, and his triumphs resonated with a surprisingly large number of people, many of whom shared their own inspiring tales of overcoming adversity. This virtual community fostered a sense of belonging and shared purpose, strengthening Neil's belief in himself and his capabilities.

The impact of sharing his progress went beyond simple encouragement. It also opened up new opportunities. A renowned aerospace engineer saw Neil's video, impressed by his innovative design and the resourcefulness he showed in overcoming his physical limitations. The engineer contacted Neil, inviting him to take part in a mentorship program focused on supporting young inventors with disabilities. This unexpected opportunity represented a significant step toward his dream, a direct result of celebrating his small victories and sharing his journey with the world.

The journey wasn't always easy, and there were moments when doubt crept in. But Neil's newfound strategy, embracing and celebrating every small step forward, gave him a way to push through those low points. He learned to appreciate the incremental progress, the small achievements that often go unnoticed. He realized that it's not just about reaching the summit, but also about savoring the views from each checkpoint along the way. The celebration of small victories wasn't just about acknowledging accomplishments; it was about nurturing a positive mindset, reinforcing his belief in himself, and maintaining the momentum necessary to pursue his audacious dream.

He continued refining his spaceship model, relentlessly pursuing perfection, even while acknowledging that true perfection is often an elusive goal. His progress, though gradual, was consistent. Each small success, a successfully soldered joint, a perfectly aligned gear, a smoothly operating mechanism, became a source of renewed energy and motivation. He had learned that true success is not measured solely by the final outcome but also by the journey itself. The countless hours spent working on his model, the challenges overcome, and the skills acquired all added up to something much bigger than just a finished project.

The celebration of these small triumphs wasn't about self-congratulation; it was about acknowledging the effort, recognizing the progress, and reinforcing the positive feedback loop that fueled his journey. It was about building resilience, strengthening his belief in his abilities, and reaffirming the unwavering support of his family, friends, and online community.

The completion of his model, therefore, was not just a single event but a culmination of many smaller accomplishments, each one a testament to his unwavering determination and his ability to overcome adversity. It was a chorus of small victories, each note played with precision and passion, composing a powerful melody of resilience and hope. Neil's journey underscored the importance of acknowledging and celebrating every step forward, no matter how small, in the pursuit of one's dreams. The path to the stars, he realized, was paved with these small, but incredibly significant, victories.

He was ready to keep going, one small victory at a time.

CHAPTER 20:

A BREAKTHROUGH

The gyroscope, the bane of his existence for weeks, spun flawlessly. A faint hum, barely audible, came from the miniature device, proof of Neil's tireless effort. He had spent countless nights hunched over his workbench, brow furrowed in concentration, his three-fingered hand carefully adjusting tiny components. He had tried different materials, tested various designs, and experimented with soldering techniques, pushing his creativity to the edge. The failures were many. Each one had been a frustrating reminder of the challenges he faced.

But every failure had taught him something. Every setback had moved him one step closer to this moment.

This wasn't just a working gyroscope. It was a symbol of how far he had come, proof of what persistence and creativity could do. He had adapted tools designed for limited dexterity, even modifying them further to suit his needs. He had come up with his own soldering method, one that gave him better control without tiring out his hand. He felt a deep pride, not just in the finished result, but in everything it had taken to get there.

The breakthrough didn't end there. The entire spaceship model had gone through a serious upgrade. He had improved the propulsion system to run more efficiently and fine-tuned the navigation by adding a compact GPS unit. He had even managed to build a basic life support system, something he hadn't imagined when he first started. And as always, he recorded everything, notes, sketches, refinements, all carefully documented in his design journal.

The new model looked nothing like the one he had built before. It was smoother, more polished, and far more advanced. A tiny world of gears, wires, and circuits now worked in sync. He ran his hand slowly along the surface of the hull, feeling the cool metal beneath his fingertips. This wasn't just a model anymore. It was his dream made real, something he had built entirely on his own.

The pride he felt was hard to describe. It wasn't loud or dramatic. It was a steady, quiet sense of self-worth, the kind that grows from knowing exactly how much work it took to get there. Building this model wasn't just about engineering. It was about proving to himself that his differences didn't define him or limit what he could accomplish. He had met obstacles head-on, dealt with failures, and kept going.

This success was more than a technical milestone. It felt personal. It was proof that determination, creativity, and belief could push through anything. He knew this wasn't the final stop. His journey was far from over. But this moment gave him a boost of confidence that would carry him further.

He carefully packed the spaceship model, his heart full of pride and excitement. He couldn't wait to share this achievement with Grandpa Joe, Maya, his parents, and his online community. He imagined their reactions, smiles, surprise, encouragement, and the thought made him grin.

He decided to create a detailed video showcasing the improved model's features and functions. He narrated the video with enthusiasm, explaining the technical aspects of his design, highlighting the challenges he overcame, and sharing his insights and experiences. He included close-up shots of the miniature gyroscope, the propulsion system, and the life support system, highlighting the intricate details of his work. He even included footage of his earlier attempts, along with the failures and the lessons he learned along the way.

He uploaded the video to his online community, expecting the feedback and encouragement he had grown accustomed to. The comments poured in, a wave of praise and admiration. People from all over the world, many with their own unique challenges, shared their stories of perseverance and resilience. The sense of community was inspiring, a reminder that he wasn't alone on his journey.

Among the comments was a message from a renowned aerospace engineer who had been following Neil's progress for some time. The engineer was particularly impressed by Neil's ingenuity and his ability to overcome his physical limitations. He offered Neil an invitation to take part in a mentorship program, a once-in-a-lifetime opportunity that could greatly accelerate Neil's progress towards his dream.

This unexpected invitation was a powerful validation of Neil's hard work and dedication. It was a testament to the power of perseverance, the importance of sharing one's journey, and the unexpected rewards that can come from celebrating small victories. Neil knew that this was a major step towards his ultimate goal. The path to space was still long, but this breakthrough had given him the confidence and the motivation to continue his extraordinary journey.

He dedicated himself to the mentorship program, absorbing the knowledge and experience of his mentor. He continued to refine his spaceship model, incorporating the new knowledge he gained. He worked tirelessly, pushing himself beyond his limits, driven by his passion and his unwavering determination. His journey, far from being over, had only just begun. This breakthrough was not an end but a new beginning, a launchpad to even greater heights.

The improved spaceship model became a symbol of his resilience, his innovation, and his unwavering belief in his own abilities. It was a constant reminder that obstacles, however daunting, could be overcome through perseverance and ingenuity. He realized that his physical differences didn't diminish his potential; they enhanced it, forcing him to develop creative solutions and pushing him to innovate in ways that others might not have considered.

The experience taught him the profound importance of celebrating every small victory, every minor achievement. These small triumphs weren't just fleeting moments of joy; they were crucial building blocks, each one strengthening his resolve and pushing him closer to his dreams. The journey to space, he knew, would be paved with both significant breakthroughs and small, incremental gains. He was ready to embrace each and every one of them. His journey was his own, unique, and inspiring. He knew that his story would inspire others, a testament to the power of dreams and the unwavering human spirit.

Chapter 21:

Sharing His Success

The video concluded, and Neil leaned back in his chair, a nervous flutter in his stomach. He'd poured his heart and soul into this presentation, meticulously showcasing every detail of his improved spaceship model. The comments began to roll in, a cascade of praise and encouragement that warmed his heart. He read each one carefully, absorbing the words of support and admiration. Many commented on the ingenuity of his design, the elegance of his solutions, and the sheer determination clear in his work. Several viewers mentioned how Neil's story had inspired them to overcome their own challenges, to pursue their dreams no matter how daunting they seemed.

Among the comments were messages from children, some with disabilities similar to his own. Their words resonated deeply with Neil. He saw reflections of his own journey in their struggles and triumphs, a shared experience of overcoming adversity. He felt a surge of empathy, a powerful connection to these young people who, like him, refused to let limitations define their potential. He responded to each message personally, offering words of encouragement, sharing his own experiences, and emphasizing the importance of perseverance.

He realized that sharing his success was as important as achieving it. His journey wasn't just about reaching for the stars; it was about inspiring others to do the same. He decided to take his efforts a step further. He created a series of short videos, each focusing on a specific aspect of his spaceship model's design. These videos were aimed at younger children, explaining complex concepts in simple, easy-to-understand terms. He incorporated animations and visual aids to make the information engaging and accessible.

He posted these videos on several educational websites and

platforms, reaching a wider audience of young aspiring scientists and engineers. The response was overwhelming. Children from all over the world reached out to Neil, sharing their own projects, asking questions about his work, and expressing their admiration for his achievements. He found himself answering emails and messages late into the night, feeling a profound sense of purpose and fulfillment.

Neil's growing confidence wasn't limited to his online interactions. He began to actively take part in local science fairs and robotics competitions. He shared his skills, mentoring younger children and helping them overcome their challenges. He taught them about problem-solving, troubleshooting, and the importance of never giving up on their dreams. He became a role model, a beacon of inspiration for those who had once felt limited by their circumstances.

At one particular science fair, a young girl approached Neil, her eyes wide with admiration. She was hesitant at first, clutching a half-finished robot in her hands. She explained that she had been struggling with the wiring, her fingers fumbling with the tiny components. She was on the verge of giving up, feeling discouraged by her difficulties. Neil patiently listened to her concerns, gently guiding her through the process and offering practical advice. He showed her different techniques, demonstrating how to adapt tools and tackle challenges with ingenuity.

With Neil's help, the young girl managed to complete her robot, a feeling of accomplishment washing over her. She beamed with pride, her frustration replaced by a newfound sense of confidence. Neil's act of kindness had not only helped her overcome a technical hurdle but had also boosted her self-esteem and belief in her abilities. It was a moment that underscored the power of mentorship and the profound impact a single act of kindness can have.

Neil continued to share his knowledge and skills, organizing workshops and online tutorials for children interested in science and engineering. He used his experience to prove that limitations don't define potential, and that creativity and innovation are crucial parts of success. He shared his own struggles and setbacks, highlighting the importance of learning from mistakes and persisting through difficulty.

He emphasized the importance of collaboration, explaining how working together, sharing ideas, and learning from one another could lead to greater achievements. He encouraged teamwork and peer support, building a vibrant community of young scientists and engineers who inspired and supported one another. He became a catalyst for a new generation of dreamers, each pursuing their passions with unwavering determination.

His work extended beyond mentoring and teaching. He collaborated with local schools and community centers to organize STEM (Science, Technology, Engineering, and Mathematics) programs, offering hands-on activities and workshops for children of all ages and abilities. He developed engaging curriculum materials, integrating his own experiences and lessons into the educational programs.

His efforts earned him recognition and accolades. He received awards and scholarships, further fueling his passion and drive. But the most rewarding part of his work was the impact it had on the lives of the children he mentored. He received countless messages from parents and teachers, expressing gratitude for the positive influence he had made.

Neil's journey had taken an unexpected turn. His original goal of space exploration had evolved into a broader mission: to inspire and empower others to pursue their dreams, regardless of their physical abilities or personal circumstances. He discovered that his true purpose was not only to reach for the stars himself but to help others reach for them too.

He started a blog to document his journey and share his insights. It quickly became a source of inspiration and encouragement for people from all walks of life. He received messages from adults as well as children, each one sharing their own stories of perseverance and passion. His story transcended age and background, forming a global community of shared hope and support.

Neil continued to refine his spaceship model, constantly seeking ways to improve its functionality and design. He learned from every setback, adapting and innovating in response to new challenges.

He viewed each failure as a learning opportunity, a step forward instead of a step back. His resilience was contagious, showing others that setbacks weren't permanent roadblocks but valuable moments that shaped growth.

He knew his journey to space might still be long and difficult, but it now felt richer and more meaningful. He realized that true achievement wasn't just about reaching his dream — it was about the lives he touched along the way. He was showing people how to dream big, believe in themselves, and never let obstacles define their limits.

His story had become a testament to the power of belief, perseverance, and the extraordinary potential inside every person, regardless of their background or challenges. What had begun as a personal dream had turned into a shared mission, powered by the energy of a community united by hope, determination, and ambition.

CHAPTER 22:

COMMUNITY SUPPORT

The local newspaper, *The Prescott Gazette*, ran a story about Neil and his extraordinary journey. The article, accompanied by a photograph of Neil proudly displaying his spaceship model, highlighted his ingenuity, perseverance, and inspiring story. The response was immediate and overwhelming. Letters poured in from across the town, expressing admiration and offering support. Many readers were moved by Neil's determination and his ability to overcome adversity.

A local hardware store, owned by Mr. Henderson, a kind-hearted man with a passion for engineering, offered to donate all the materials Neil would need for his future projects. Mr. Henderson, deeply touched by Neil's story, saw in him a reflection of his own youthful ambition. He remembered his own struggles as a young boy, his dreams often overshadowed by financial constraints. He wanted to ensure that Neil wouldn't face the same limitations. The offer wasn't just about materials; it was a gesture of faith in Neil's potential, a belief in his unwavering spirit.

The Prescott Community Center, known for its vibrant atmosphere and diverse programs, offered Neil free access to their workshop facilities. This was a big chance. The workshop was equipped with advanced tools and equipment that Neil had only ever dreamed of using. It provided him with a dedicated space to work on his projects without distractions, surrounded by a supportive community of artisans and hobbyists. The center's staff became a source of encouragement and friendship, constantly providing Neil with aid and celebrating his achievements.

The local library, a haven for bookworms and knowledge-seekers, organized a special book reading and Q&A session featuring Neil. Children from all over the town came to the event, eager to hear Neil's story and learn from his experiences. Neil talked about his journey, his setbacks, and his wins, inspiring the young crowd with his message of sticking with your goals and believing in yourself. The librarians, impressed by Neil's commitment to STEM education, dedicated a section of the library to space exploration and offered Neil the opportunity to curate a collection of books on the subject.

Word of Neil's story spread beyond Prescott. A renowned aerospace engineer, Dr. Amelia Hernandez, read the newspaper article and was captivated by Neil's determination. She reached out to Neil and offered to mentor him. Dr. Hernandez, a pioneer in her field, had faced her own challenges throughout her career, and she saw in Neil a kindred spirit, a young innovator with the potential to make significant contributions to the field of aerospace engineering. Her guidance provided Neil with invaluable insights and a network of professionals in the aerospace industry.

Financial support also began pouring in. A local fundraising campaign was organized, raising a substantial amount of money to support Neil's projects and his future education. The whole town seemed to rally around him, showing not just generosity, but real belief in his talent. The donations came in various forms: large and small contributions, all reflecting the community's collective desire to help Neil reach for the stars.

Beyond the material support, the most valuable gift Neil received was the unwavering emotional support from his community. He felt a profound sense of belonging, a feeling of being embraced and cherished by those who believed in him. He was no longer just a boy with a dream; he was a member of a community that rallied behind him, providing him with the strength and courage he needed to pursue his aspirations.

Neighbors stopped by to offer words of encouragement, share stories of their own challenges overcome, and simply to offer a listening ear. Children in his neighborhood would often join him in his workshop, their curiosity piqued by his inventions and their admiration for his tenacity. These interactions provided

Neil with a sense of connection and belonging, reminding him that he was not alone in his journey.

His grandpa, a constant source of inspiration, became even more involved, sharing stories of his own life and how he overcame obstacles. The bond between them deepened, strengthening Neil's resolve and reminding him of the enduring power of family support.

His grandpa's wisdom, shared over cups of warm cocoa on cold evenings, served as a constant source of encouragement and strength.

The school principal, moved by Neil's story, arranged for special workshops and lectures related to space exploration at the school. Neil became a guest lecturer, sharing his knowledge and inspiring younger students. His story became part of the school's curriculum, a testament to the power of perseverance and the importance of pursuing one's dreams, regardless of the challenges.

Neil's journey transformed the community. It fostered a sense of unity and shared purpose, reminding everyone of the importance of supporting each other and believing in the potential of every individual. The community's collective action became a powerful example of the positive impact that a supportive environment can have on a young person's life.

Neil's story became a symbol of hope and inspiration for the entire town. It served as a reminder that dreams, no matter how ambitious, can be achieved with perseverance, hard work, and the unwavering support of a caring community. The collective effort to help Neil pursue his passion demonstrated the power of community spirit, highlighting the importance of fostering inclusivity and celebrating the unique talents and aspirations of each individual.

The impact didn't stop there. Inspired by Neil's story, other children with disabilities found the courage to pursue their own passions. The community's response to Neil sparked a renewed focus on inclusive education and providing resources for children with diverse needs. Local businesses and organizations started initiatives to support children with disabilities, ensuring that they had the opportunities they deserved to reach their full potential.

Even the local government took notice. Seeing the way the town had responded, they committed to improving access to public spaces and creating more inclusive programs. Neil's determination, combined with the town's support, had started something big.

Neil's journey continued, but it was no longer a solitary one. He had a community behind him, a network of supporters providing him with the resources, encouragement, and love he needed to pursue his dreams. His story served as a powerful reminder that even the most ambitious dreams can be realized with perseverance, determination, and the invaluable support of a caring community.

The journey to space stayed his ultimate goal, but the journey itself, filled with the love and support of his community, was already an incredible achievement. His story became a timeless tale of courage, resilience, and the extraordinary power of belief, shared and strengthened by the bonds of community. It was a testament to the idea that while dreams may take flight individually, they soar highest when carried by the collective strength of those who believe.

CHAPTER 23:

OVERCOMING SELF-DOUBT

The accolades continued to pour in, but amidst the whirlwind of success, a quiet battle raged within Neil. It wasn't the physical challenges of his shorter arm and three-fingered hand that troubled him now; it was a different kind of obstacle, a more insidious enemy: self-doubt. It crept in subtly at first, a whisper in the back of his mind, questioning his capabilities. He would be working meticulously on a new spaceship model, a complex design incorporating intricate details and innovative mechanisms, and suddenly, a wave of uncertainty would wash over him.

"What if I'm not good enough?" he'd wonder, staring at his half-finished creation. "What if I fail? What if all this attention was a mistake?" The doubt gnawed at his confidence, threatening to unravel the hard-won progress he'd made. He'd find himself comparing his work to the intricate models he'd seen in museums, feeling a pang of inadequacy. The fear of failure loomed large, casting a shadow over his enthusiasm. His normally nimble fingers would falter, the tools feeling clumsy and unfamiliar in his grasp. He'd spend hours staring at the incomplete project, unable to muster the energy to continue.

These moments of self-doubt were surprisingly frequent. They would strike at the most unexpected times; during presentations, amidst the encouraging applause, even while receiving the heartwarming words of his grandpa. He'd catch his reflection in the glass of a window and find himself scrutinizing his hand, the physical difference a stark reminder of his perceived limitations. The negativity wasn't always loud; sometimes it was a quiet, persistent hum, a constant background noise that threatened to drown out the positive chorus of his success.

One evening, as he sat hunched over his workbench, wrestling with a particularly stubborn piece of circuitry, the self-doubt struck with particular force. Tears welled up in his eyes. He felt overwhelmed, the weight of expectations pressing down on him. He felt like he was failing, not only himself but also the community that had embraced him with such unwavering support. The pressure to succeed felt unbearable.

His grandpa, sensing his distress, gently approached him. He didn't try to dismiss Neil's feelings; instead, he sat beside him, his hand resting reassuringly on Neil's shoulder. "Tell me what's troubling you, my boy," he said softly, his voice a calm balm to Neil's frayed nerves.

Neil, overwhelmed by emotion, poured out his heart. He spoke of his fears, his doubts, his anxieties about letting everyone down. He confessed his apprehension about his capabilities, his worry that he wouldn't live up to the expectations that had been placed upon him. Despite all the successes, he still felt fundamentally inadequate.

His grandpa listened patiently, his eyes filled with understanding and compassion. When Neil had finished, his grandpa smiled gently. "Neil," he began, "self-doubt is a visitor, not a resident. It comes to everyone, even the bravest among us. It's a normal part of life, a human experience. But you don't have to let it set up camp and take over."

He continued, "Remember all the times you've overcome challenges? Remember the countless hours you spent designing and building your spaceships? Think about the perseverance, the ingenuity, and the sheer determination you've shown repeatedly? Those aren't the actions of someone who is incapable. They are the actions of someone who is strong, capable, and remarkably resilient."

His grandpa pointed to a shelf laden with Neil's spaceship models, each one a testament to his skill and creativity. "Look at all these amazing creations, Neil," he said. "Each one a triumph, a victory over obstacles, both big and small. These are not the creations of a failure, my boy. They are the work of a dreamer, an inventor, a visionary."

He then spoke about the community's support, not just as material aid but as a testament to their belief in Neil. "The people of Prescott didn't rally around you because they saw a boy who might fail. They saw a boy who was determined to succeed, a boy with courage, passion, and a heart filled with dreams. They believed in you, Neil. That belief is powerful."

His grandpa's words resonated deeply with Neil. He began to see his self-doubt not as a reflection of his abilities, but as a fleeting emotion, a temporary cloud blocking out the bright sun of his accomplishments. He realized that self-doubt was a natural human experience and that acknowledging it, rather than fighting it, was the first step towards overcoming it.

From that day on, Neil developed strategies to manage his self-doubt. When the whispers of negativity started, he would actively counter them with affirmations of his strengths. He'd make a list of his achievements, big and small, and read it whenever the doubt crept in. He would remind himself of the support he had, picturing the faces of his friends, family, and the wider Prescott community who believed in him. He would take a moment to appreciate the progress he'd made, no matter how small.

He also learned to ask for help when he needed it. He wouldn't hesitate to approach Dr. Hernandez for guidance or Mr. Henderson for advice. He shared his struggles with his friends, realizing that his vulnerability didn't diminish him but rather deepened his bonds with them. They shared their own moments of self-doubt, creating a space of mutual understanding and support.

His confidence grew gradually, not in leaps and bounds, but in steady, incremental steps. He learned that progress wasn't always linear; there would be setbacks, moments of hesitation, but these were simply opportunities to learn and grow. He started to view challenges not as threats, but as opportunities for growth, for refining his skills and pushing the boundaries of his abilities.

The journey wasn't always easy; the self-doubt would occasionally reappear, but Neil had developed the resilience and the tools to manage it. He'd learned to see it not as a sign of failure, but as a natural part of the process, a reminder that even the strongest among us have moments of weakness. And it was in those moments of vulnerability that he found the greatest strength—the strength to persevere, to believe in himself, and to continue reaching for the stars.

His final project, a sophisticated lunar rover designed for navigating challenging terrains, was a culmination of his journey. It was a masterpiece of engineering, incorporating innovative designs and technological marvels. While working on the rover, the old familiar doubts did appear, but he faced them with a newfound confidence. He acknowledged them, allowing them to pass through him without taking root. He focused on the present task, drawing strength from the unwavering support of his community and the belief in himself that had been cultivated over time.

The unveiling of the lunar rover was a resounding success. The intricate design, the meticulous craftsmanship, the sheer innovation—it all spoke to Neil's exceptional talent and dedication. The community erupted in applause, their admiration palpable, their pride overflowing. This time, Neil felt different. The applause felt warm, but it didn't define him. He felt a sense of inner peace, a quiet confidence that resonated far more deeply than any external validation. He had not only built an amazing rover but had also built an unshakeable belief in himself, a belief forged in the crucible of self-doubt and strengthened by the unwavering support of a loving community.

His journey to space was still ahead, but he was ready. He was ready to face any challenges, armed with his skills, his resilience, and the unwavering belief in the power of his own dreams. His journey had become a testament not only to the power of belief, but also to the remarkable capacity of the human spirit to overcome even its most formidable internal adversaries. The journey, after all, was as important as the destination. Neil, more than ever, knew the incredible strength he carried within himself—a strength found not only in his ability to create, but in his ability to conquer the often-unspoken battles fought within his own heart and mind.

CHAPTER 24:

EMBRACING UNIQUENESS

The unveiling of the lunar rover was a triumphant moment, not just for Neil but for the entire town of Prescott. The celebratory atmosphere crackled with excitement, the air thick with the scent of freshly baked cookies and the joyful chatter of the crowd. Neil, standing beside his creation, felt a surge of pride that went far beyond the accolades and applause. This wasn't just about the rover; it was about the journey, the challenges overcome, the self-doubt conquered, and the belief in himself that had carried him through it all.

He looked at his hands, the shorter arm and three-fingered hand that had once been a source of insecurity, and now saw them as badges of honor, symbols of his resilience and ingenuity. He understood that his difference hadn't been a limitation; it had been a catalyst, pushing him to find innovative solutions, to think creatively, and to develop a unique perspective that others lacked. The way he manipulated tools, the way he designed his spaceships and the rover, were all a testament to this unique approach, a way of thinking shaped by his difference.

Dr. Hernandez, beaming with pride, stepped forward to address the crowd. She spoke of Neil's exceptional talent, his unwavering dedication, and the innovative designs that had revolutionized lunar rover technology. She highlighted not just the technical marvel of the rover, but the inspirational journey that had led to its creation, a journey built on self-discovery, resilience, and the determination to believe in oneself despite challenges.

Her words resonated deeply with the assembled crowd, many wiping away tears of emotion and pride. Neil's journey had become a symbol of hope and inspiration, proving that differences are not weaknesses but rather a source of unique strengths. It showed that true potential wasn't defined by physical attributes but by the unshakable spirit within. Neil's story became a powerful narrative, a testament to the importance of believing in oneself and the transformative power of embracing one's unique identity.

Following the official ceremony, Neil spent hours interacting with the community, sharing stories, answering questions, and inspiring others with his journey. Children, particularly, were drawn to him, their eyes wide with wonder and admiration. In many of them, he saw his younger self — the child who felt different, who didn't quite fit in. He shared his story, not as a boastful tale of achievement, but as a message of hope and encouragement, emphasizing that their differences were their strengths, their uniqueness was their power.

He spent time talking to a young girl with a noticeable limp, reassuring her that her differences would not define her potential. He spoke to a boy who stammered, assuring him that his ability to communicate would only become stronger with perseverance and self-belief. He spoke to children from diverse backgrounds, showing them that their cultures, languages, and traditions were what made their identities rich and diverse.

Neil realized that his journey had taken on a life of its own, transcending the realm of personal achievement to become a message of hope and inclusion. He understood that his experience resonated deeply because it touched upon a universal truth: everyone, at some point in their lives, will grapple with self-doubt and feelings of inadequacy. But it was the ability to overcome these challenges, to embrace one's unique identity and believe in oneself, that truly defined success.

His journey had become an anthem for self-acceptance, diversity, and the power of belief. His story, once a deeply personal narrative, had transformed into a beacon of hope for countless others, showing that differences can fuel creativity, originality, and new ways of thinking. He saw himself as a bridge, connecting people, uniting them in their shared humanity and their unique identities.

His grandpa, seeing him from a distance, felt an immense sense of pride. He had always believed in Neil, but seeing his grandson not only achieve his dreams but also inspire others to believe in themselves was an even greater joy. He knew that Neil's impact would extend far beyond Prescott, reaching communities across the globe. Neil's story wasn't just about space exploration; it was about the human spirit's capacity for resilience, growth, and the transformative power of believing in oneself.

As the day drew to a close, Neil found himself reflecting on his journey. He had come a long way from the boy who had hidden his hand in his pockets, afraid of judgment. He had transformed self-doubt into self-belief, insecurity into confidence, and limitations into opportunities. He had not only achieved his personal dreams but had also become an inspiration for others to embrace their unique selves and believe in their incredible potential.

He understood now that his difference wasn't something to be hidden or ashamed of; it was his superpower, the very thing that had shaped his unique perspective, his creativity, and his resilience. It was the source of his strength, his originality, his very essence. He had come to appreciate that true strength wasn't about conformity; it was about embracing one's uniqueness, celebrating one's individual identity, and using it as a catalyst for creativity and innovation.

The journey to space still beckoned, but it was no longer just a personal aspiration. It had become a symbol, a testament to the power of belief, the importance of self-acceptance, and the incredible capacity of the human spirit to overcome any obstacle. He knew that the challenges ahead would be formidable, but he also knew he had the strength, the resilience, and the unwavering belief in himself to overcome them.

The physical differences, once a source of insecurity, now served as a reminder of his journey, of the struggles overcome, and of the incredible strength he had discovered within himself. He looked at his hand, the shorter arm and three-fingered hand, and saw not limitations, but symbols of his unique path, his special perspective, and his unparalleled capacity for creativity.

Neil's story became a legend in Prescott, a story passed down from generation to generation, inspiring countless children to embrace their differences, believe in their dreams, and strive for their potential, regardless of the challenges they faced. His journey served as a potent reminder that true strength lies not in conforming to societal expectations, but in celebrating individuality, embracing uniqueness, and harnessing the power of belief to achieve the seemingly impossible. His story became a testament to the extraordinary power of the human spirit to overcome adversity and achieve greatness, even against the greatest of odds. His journey to space would undoubtedly be a journey of incredible adventure, but the journey of self-discovery and self-acceptance had already brought him to his ultimate destination: a place of unwavering self-belief and profound contentment. And that, he knew, was a journey worth celebrating.

CHAPTER 25:

INSPIRING OTHERS

The news of Neil's lunar rover spread like wildfire, not just through Prescott but across the country. News channels featured him, highlighting his ingenuity and the story behind his creation. His journey resonated with people from all walks of life, sparking a sense of hope and possibility. Almost overnight, Neil became a role model, a symbol of inspiration for countless children and adults who felt different, overlooked, or underestimated.

Letters began pouring into the town hall, addressed simply to "Neil, the Space Boy." Children shared their own stories of struggles and dreams, many of them echoing Neil's experiences. A young girl from a small rural town wrote about her ambition to become a veterinarian, despite financial hardship. A boy from a bustling city confessed his passion for astrophysics, even though he was often bullied for being quiet. A girl with Down syndrome described her dream of becoming an artist, proudly enclosing colorful drawings alongside her letter. Each message was proof of the power of Neil's story, lighting sparks of hope in hearts that had once believed their dreams were out of reach.

Neil, overwhelmed but deeply moved, tried to answer as many letters as he could. His responses were personal and heartfelt. He encouraged children to chase their passions, reminding them that their differences were their strengths and that their unique perspectives were their greatest assets. He stressed that the dream itself was important, but so was the journey, the resilience, the self-belief, and the lessons learned along the way. Setbacks, he wrote, were inevitable, but giving up was never an option.

These letters were more than just words on paper. They were acts of empathy, understanding, and genuine support. Neil didn't promise easy solutions or instant success. Instead, he shared his own moments of fear, self-doubt, and the times he nearly walked away. He told them it was okay to stumble, to feel unsure, and even to be scared. What mattered most was the choice to stand back up, to keep moving, and to believe in themselves despite the odds.

His sincerity resonated deeply. Speaking from the heart, he shared what he had learned: the value of perseverance, the importance of collaboration, the beauty of individuality, and the life-changing power of self-belief. He urged children to discover their own "superpowers" — the strengths that set them apart. He reminded them that their differences were not flaws but remarkable qualities that made them extraordinary.

Soon, schools began inviting Neil to speak. He stood before auditoriums packed with children, their eyes wide with curiosity and excitement. He spoke not as a scientist or an engineer, but as a boy who had dared to dream big and had turned what others saw as limitations into strengths. He told stories from his journey, recalling the challenges he had faced, the moments of discouragement, and the determination that had carried him through. He shared his sketches, models, and research notes, letting the students see the effort and passion behind his achievements.

These talks were not formal lectures. They were lively, interactive sessions filled with questions, laughter, and honest conversations. Children told him about their own dreams, their worries, and their fears. Neil listened closely, answering with encouragement, understanding, and reassurance. He reminded them that every path was unique, every goal personal, and that their potential was far greater than they realized. He emphasized that success was not only about the outcome but also about the belief and persistence shown along the way.

Neil's influence quickly spread beyond classrooms. He inspired art projects, science fairs, and community programs focused on inclusion and celebrating differences. Children formed science clubs, built their own robots, and wrote their own stories, motivated by his belief in the power of dreams. Even adults were moved; teachers, parents, and community leaders began embracing his message of empowerment and acceptance.

Neil's story became more than a tale of space exploration. It was a reminder of the human spirit's ability to grow, adapt, and overcome. It celebrated the strength that comes from self-acceptance and the courage to embrace one's identity. He became a beacon for anyone facing obstacles, whether those were physical challenges, learning differences, financial struggles, or feelings of isolation. His message was clear: limitations are often self-imposed, and potential is limitless.

Wanting to give back, Neil founded "Reaching for the Stars," a program supporting underprivileged children who dreamed of working in STEM. The foundation offered scholarships, mentoring, and resources to help young people overcome barriers and follow their passions. What began as his personal journey had grown into a global movement, inspiring millions to trust in their abilities and push toward their goals. Neil showed that obstacles could be turned into opportunities for creativity, innovation, and discovering one's own strengths.

His influence kept growing, reaching far beyond personal success. He inspired people everywhere to challenge stereotypes, rethink what it meant to succeed, and embrace the power of self-belief. His story traveled well beyond Prescott, reaching communities worldwide, sparking hope, and encouraging countless people to aim for their own dreams, no matter how distant they seemed. He proved that success is not about fitting into expectations but about standing proudly in one's individuality and using that uniqueness to achieve the extraordinary.

Neil's journey was far from finished. The next chapter, his mission to space, was only just beginning. And the world was watching, ready to believe in the boy who had dared to dream beyond the stars.

CHAPTER 26:

THE FINAL LAUNCH

The day of the launch dawned bright and clear, a perfect mirror to the excitement bubbling in Neil's heart. His final spaceship model, a magnificent creation of polished wood, gleaming metal, and intricate wiring, sat poised on the launchpad, a structure the town had built together right in the square. It wasn't just a model; it was a symbol, a testament to his unwavering spirit, and his relentless pursuit of a dream that once seemed impossibly distant.

The town square was transformed. Banners fluttered in the gentle breeze, proclaiming "Neil's Great Launch!" Children, their faces painted with stars and planets, chattered excitedly, their voices blending into a vibrant symphony of anticipation. Parents, their eyes filled with pride and wonder, stood beside them, a quiet show of the support that had fueled Neil's journey from the start. The air hummed with a palpable energy, a blend of joy, hope, and the shared thrill of witnessing something extraordinary.

The launchpad itself was a marvel of community collaboration. Mr. Henderson, the town's carpenter, had crafted the sturdy wooden base. Mrs. Gable, known for her artistic flair, had painted a breathtaking mural depicting Neil's journey, from his initial sketches to the final model. Even the local bakery contributed, creating miniature spaceships out of gingerbread, a delicious symbol of the sweet success Neil was about to celebrate.

Neil, dressed in a custom-made spacesuit crafted by his ingenious grandfather, stood beside his creation, a nervous smile playing on his lips. He felt a surge of gratitude, not just for the support he'd received, but for the journey itself. The challenges, the setbacks, the moments of self-doubt had all shaped him, forging a resilience and self-belief he never knew he possessed.

His grandfather, his eyes twinkling with pride, placed a hand on his shoulder. "Ready for liftoff, kid?" he asked softly, his voice thick with emotion.

Neil nodded, his heart pounding fast and steady with both nerves and excitement. He took a deep breath, the crisp morning air filling his lungs, and looked out at the assembled crowd. Their faces, a mosaic of hope and admiration, filled him with a warmth that transcended the chill of the autumn morning.

The countdown began, echoing through the square, each number a beat of anticipation leading to the decisive moment.

"Ten... nine... eight..." The voices grew louder, more insistent, their collective energy pushing Neil's excitement to its peak. "... three... two... one..."

And then, with a gentle hiss of compressed air, Neil's spaceship model soared into the sky. A collective gasp swept through the crowd, followed by a thunderous applause. The spaceship, propelled by a cleverly designed system of balloons and miniature rockets, ascended gracefully, a beacon of hope against the azure canvas. It climbed higher and higher, a tiny speck against the vast expanse of the sky, finally disappearing into the clouds.

The launch wasn't just a physical event; it was a powerful metaphor for Neil's journey. It symbolized his ascent from doubt and insecurity to self-acceptance and unwavering belief. The collective cheer wasn't just for the spaceship; it was a celebration of Neil's resilience, his creativity, and his refusal to let his physical difference define him.

The celebration continued long after the spaceship vanished from sight. Food was shared, stories were told, and laughter echoed through the square. Neil, surrounded by his friends, family, and the entire community, felt a sense of overwhelming joy and belonging.

He understood now that his journey wasn't just about reaching a destination, like space itself, but about the transformative power of the journey.

That evening, as the sun dipped below the horizon, casting a warm golden glow over Prescott, Neil sat on his porch, gazing at the star-studded sky. He felt a profound sense of peace, a quiet satisfaction that went beyond the accomplishment of launching his spaceship. He'd proven to himself, and to the world, that limitations were not boundaries, that differences were strengths, and that the most extraordinary journeys begin with a single, unwavering dream.

His journey to space, in the literal sense, was still a long way off. He had taken the first step, not just in building his spaceship models, but in believing in himself and his capabilities. He'd learned that true success wasn't just about reaching a destination; it was about the strength gained, the lessons learned, the connections forged, and the unwavering belief in oneself along the way.

The letters continued to arrive, each one a testament to the ripple effect of his story. Children, inspired by Neil's journey, shared their own aspirations, dreams of becoming doctors, artists, engineers, and astronauts. Their words weren't just about their own ambitions; they were about the hope Neil had ignited, the belief he'd instilled in the power of dreams, no matter how ambitious or seemingly impossible.

Neil's influence extended far beyond Prescott. His story was featured in national newspapers and magazines, his interviews broadcast on television and radio. He became a symbol of hope and inspiration, not just for children with physical differences, but for anyone who had ever felt limited by their circumstances, their background, or their self-doubt.

His "Reaching for the Stars" foundation flourished, providing support and resources to countless children pursuing their dreams in STEM fields. He traveled extensively, speaking at schools and conferences, sharing his message of self-belief and resilience. He showed them his sketches, his models, his research notes, not as artifacts of accomplishment, but as tangible representations of his journey, his challenges, and his unwavering dedication.

Neil's story wasn't just about space exploration; it became a powerful narrative about the human spirit's capacity to overcome adversity, to embrace individuality, and to find strength in vulnerability. It was a testament to the transformative power of believing in oneself, of pursuing one's dreams with unwavering determination, and of finding fulfillment not just in the destination, but in the enriching journey itself.

Years later, Neil did indeed travel to space. But his true journey, the one that had transformed him and inspired millions, began long before he ever set foot on a rocket. It began with a simple dream, a belief in himself, and the unwavering support of a community that believed in him too. His story, etched in the annals of human spirit, served as a beacon of hope, a reminder that every individual, regardless of their perceived limitations, has the potential to reach for the stars and achieve the seemingly impossible. His journey, far from over, continued to inspire, shaping countless lives and redefining the very meaning of extraordinary. The launch of his model spaceship was just the beginning, a symbolic representation of a far greater journey of self-discovery and the boundless potential of the human spirit. The world watched, not just for his space travel, but for the continuing saga of the boy who dared to dream beyond the stars and inspired everyone else to do the same.

CHAPTER 27:

REFLECTING ON THE JOURNEY

The cheering crowd slowly dispersed, leaving behind a quiet stillness in the town square. Neil, however, felt anything but quiet. A wave of emotion washed over him; a potent cocktail of exhilaration, gratitude, and a profound sense of accomplishment. The launch of his model spaceship wasn't just a symbolic victory; it was a tangible representation of years of hard work, steady perseverance, and believing in himself even when others doubted him.

He sat on the now-empty launchpad, the scent of freshly cut wood and paint still lingering in the air. He touched the smooth surface of the wooden base, each grain a testament to the meticulous craftsmanship of Mr. Henderson, whose hands were rough from years of work but steady enough to help bring Neil's dream to life. He traced the vibrant lines of Mrs. Gable's mural, a visual journey chronicling his own path, from hesitant sketches to a breathtaking model ready for liftoff. Every detail, every element, every person who contributed stood for a crucial piece of his puzzle, a testament to the power of community support.

His grandfather's words echoed in his mind: "It's not about the destination, Neil, it's about the journey." At the time, he understood the sentiment, but now, sitting amidst the remnants of the celebration, he truly grasped its meaning. The challenges he'd faced, the moments of self-doubt, the days when giving up felt easier than continuing, the physical limitations that had once seemed impossible to overcome; these weren't roadblocks to avoid but stepping stones on his path. They had shaped him, molded him, and ultimately made him stronger.

He thought back to the countless hours spent hunched over his workbench, meticulously crafting each piece of his spaceship. The frustration, the moments of near abandonment, the countless failed attempts — they had all been part of the process, refining his skills, honing his creativity, and pushing him beyond what he thought possible. He recalled the late nights spent poring over books on astrophysics, aerospace engineering, and space exploration, his smaller hand carefully sketching diagrams and copying equations into his notebook. These weren't just acts of preparation; they were proof of his determination, a reminder that his dream was worth chasing no matter how far away it seemed.

He remembered the times he'd been teased, the whispers and stares he'd endured because of his shorter arm and three-fingered hand. Those moments, once heavy with embarrassment, now felt distant, overshadowed by the pride of what he had achieved. He had turned what others saw as weaknesses into strengths, using his unique perspective to solve problems in ways no one else could, proving that limitations were not boundaries, but opportunities for creativity and ingenuity. He had learned to see his difference not as a flaw, but as a kind of superpower, a unique way of looking at the world.

The letters he'd received since the launch flooded his memory; letters from children who, inspired by his story, had begun to embrace their own dreams, no matter how unusual or challenging they seemed. A young girl who loved coding, a boy fascinated by marine biology, a girl who wanted to be a writer; their stories echoed his own, proof that one person's journey could spark so many others. He was no longer just a boy with a dream; he was a spark that lit other people's dreams, a reminder that hard work and belief could take you far.

His "Reaching for the Stars" foundation, born from his desire to share his journey and inspire others, had blossomed into a vibrant hub of support and encouragement for young people pursuing STEM fields. He envisioned a future where every child, no matter their background or abilities, had the chance to explore their passions, to test their limits, and to discover the magic hidden inside them. His foundation was more than just a charity; it was a legacy, a living reminder that one dream could grow into something bigger than anyone imagined.

He thought of his grandfather, the source of his confidence. His grandfather's words, encouragement, and quiet support had been the base on which Neil built everything. He had taught Neil not only about spaceships and rockets but also about perseverance, resilience, and the strength inside the human spirit. The lessons weren't just about space travel; they were about life — facing challenges, celebrating victories, and seeing the beauty in the journey.

Neil stood, stretching his arms toward the twilight sky. The stars, his lifelong companions, twinkled above him, almost like they were nodding back at him. He realized that the journey to space, in a literal sense, was still ahead of him. But the most important journey, the one where he discovered himself, accepted who he was, overcame fear, and inspired others, was already complete. He had not just launched a model spaceship; he had launched himself, beyond old limits, into a new version of who he could be.

His journey was far from over. There were still mountains to climb, challenges to face, and places he'd never been. He faced the future with a stronger heart, a deep sense of gratitude, and the belief that dreams were worth chasing. He knew now that success wasn't just about getting to the finish line; it was about what you learned, who you met, and how you grew along the way. And with that truth in his mind, Neil would keep reaching for the stars, in every way possible, showing others that sometimes, the journey itself is the real prize.

CHAPTER 28:

CELEBRATING SUCCESS

The town square buzzed with bright, excited energy, a kaleidoscope of colors and sounds painting a vivid picture of celebration. Balloons bobbed playfully in the gentle breeze, their vibrant hues matching the joyful expressions on the faces of the gathered crowd. The air crackled with excitement, a palpable sense of shared accomplishment that enveloped everyone present. Neil, standing at the center of it all, felt a warmth spread through him, a feeling far exceeding the comfortable temperature of the late summer evening. This wasn't just a celebration of a model rocket launch; it was a celebration of a journey, a testament to unwavering determination, and a powerful demonstration of the human spirit's resilience.

Tables laden with an array of delicious treats overflowed with homemade cookies, cakes, and pies, their tempting aromas mingling with the sweet scent of freshly popped popcorn. Laughter echoed through the square, a harmonious blend of joyous exclamations and cheerful chatter. Children, their faces lit up with wonder and excitement, chased each other playfully, their energy infectious, mirroring the overall jubilant atmosphere. Parents watched with pride, their smiles reflecting the sheer delight of seeing such a heartwarming communal celebration.

Mr. Henderson, his hands calloused but his eyes twinkling with pride, beamed at Neil. He had played an integral role in the creation of the model spaceship, his skilled hands transforming Neil's meticulous plans into a breathtaking reality. He watched as Neil interacted with the crowd, his natural ease and genuine warmth making him the focal point of the celebration. Mr. Henderson felt a surge of pride not only in Neil's accomplishment but also for the strong, supportive community they had fostered.

He knew that this celebration was as much a testament to their collective efforts as it was to Neil's individual triumph.

Mrs. Gable, the artist whose mural graced the side of the launchpad, stood nearby, her heart swelling with emotion. Her vibrant artwork, a visual chronicle of Neil's journey, had captured the essence of his determination and the steady support of his community. She saw the children's fascinated reactions to her mural, their eyes wide with wonder as they traced the path of Neil's progress, from tentative sketches to the triumphant launch. The mural, she realized, had become more than art; it was a powerful symbol of hope and inspiration. It served as a reminder that dreams, no matter how bold, could be achieved with perseverance and the support of others.

The mayor, a man known for his practical demeanor, stood with a genuine smile, his usual stern expression replaced by heartfelt joy. He delivered a heartfelt speech, praising Neil's achievement and the community's steady support. His words resonated deeply with the crowd, underscoring the significance of collective effort and the power of shared dreams. He emphasized that Neil's journey was not just an individual triumph, but a testament to the strength and unity of their town, showing the profound impact of collective action and encouragement.

He spoke of the "Reaching for the Stars" foundation, Neil's initiative to inspire other children to pursue their dreams, highlighting its growing impact in the community.

The best part of the celebration was undoubtedly the unveiling of a plaque commemorating Neil's achievement. Engraved with the words "Reaching for the Stars: Neil's Journey," the plaque was affixed to the launchpad, serving as a lasting reminder of Neil's remarkable accomplishment. The crowd erupted in applause as Neil, his eyes shining with emotion, unveiled the plaque. The inscription was not just an acknowledgment of Neil's achievement, but also a symbol of inspiration, a beacon of hope for those who dared to dream, regardless of the challenges they faced. The inscription served as a powerful reminder of the potential within each individual and the importance of reaching for one's dreams.

As the sun dipped below the horizon, casting a warm golden glow over the town square, the celebration began to wind down. Yet, the feeling of joy and accomplishment lingered in the air, a warm and tangible presence that enveloped everyone present. The memories of shared laughter, heartfelt conversations, and collective rejoicing would forever be etched in the minds of those who had witnessed this exceptional event. It was a celebration not just of Neil's success, but of the power of community, the strength of the human spirit, and the unwavering belief in the power of dreams.

Neil, surrounded by his family, friends, and the community that had embraced him, felt a deep sense of gratitude and belonging. The warmth of the community's support washed over him, reaffirming the significance of their collective effort in achieving his milestone. He realized that his journey to space, both literal and metaphorical, was an ongoing odyssey, but he was not alone. He carried with him the steady encouragement of his community, a bond forged through shared dreams and collective aspirations.

The celebration concluded with the release of hundreds of glowing lanterns into the twilight sky, their gentle ascent creating a mesmerizing spectacle of floating lights. Each lantern represented a dream, a hope, or a wish for the future, and their collective glow was a powerful symbol of shared aspirations. As the lanterns drifted into the night sky, casting their ethereal light against the backdrop of twinkling stars, Neil felt a profound sense of contentment and peace. He knew his journey was far from over; it was merely the beginning of a much larger adventure. But he also knew that he was not alone on this journey, his path illuminated by the unwavering support of his family, friends, and a community that had wholeheartedly embraced his dream. He had reached for the stars, and in doing so, he had also ignited a spark of hope in the hearts of others.

The following days were filled with a whirlwind of activity. Interviews, articles, and documentaries chronicled Neil's remarkable journey, spreading his story far and wide. Letters flooded in, not just from children inspired by his resilience and determination but also from adults who found fresh inspiration in his story. The "Reaching for the Stars" foundation blossomed into a vibrant community initiative, extending support and encouragement to countless children pursuing STEM fields, regardless of their background or physical abilities. Neil's story transcended its local significance; it became a global symbol of hope and inspiration.

One of the most touching responses Neil received came from a young girl named Maria, who had been born with a similar physical difference. Maria's letter described how Neil's journey had inspired her to pursue her own dreams of becoming an astronaut. She wrote about the challenges she had faced, the moments of self-doubt, and the way Neil's story had given her the courage to believe in herself and her potential. Maria's story became a powerful testament to the far-reaching impact of Neil's inspirational journey. Her words were a powerful reminder that the true measure of Neil's success was not merely the launch of his model spaceship, but the lives he had touched and the dreams he had ignited in others.

The celebration wasn't just a one-time event; it marked a turning point. The community continued to rally around Neil, providing ongoing support for his foundation and inspiring countless others to pursue their dreams, however unconventional or challenging they may seem. Neil's journey became a living testament to the transformative power of a single dream, a single act of belief, and the enduring strength of the human spirit. He had proven that limitations do not define potential, and that with perseverance and the support of others, even the most audacious dreams could be realized. The journey, he realized, had only just begun, and he was ready for whatever challenges lay ahead, armed with the lessons he had learned, the support he had received, and the unwavering belief in the power of his dreams. The celebrations, both big and small, continued. Each was a testament to the journey, not the destination. The journey was a constellation, and each milestone was a brightly shining star.

CHAPTER 29:

FUTURE ASPIRATIONS

The celebratory glow hadn't faded entirely from the town square before Neil found himself immersed in new challenges, new projects, and new aspirations. The model rocket launch, the plaque unveiling, and the outpouring of community support had all been exhilarating, a powerful validation of his journey. For Neil, it wasn't a finish line; it was a launching pad for even bigger dreams.

His initial goal, the creation and launch of his model rocket, had been a tangible representation of his aspirations. It had served as a powerful symbol, a beacon guiding him through years of self-doubt and relentless pursuit. Now, with that goal carried out, a new horizon of possibilities stretched before him. He wasn't content to rest on his laurels; the momentum of his journey propelled him forward.

He began to delve deeper into the world of astrophysics, devouring books and scientific papers with the same energy he had previously dedicated to building his spaceship. He spent hours poring over complex equations, unraveling the mysteries of celestial mechanics, and immersing himself in the intricacies of rocket propulsion. His three-fingered hand, once perceived as a limitation, became a testament to his adaptability. He developed innovative techniques to handle intricate tools, finding inventive solutions to challenges that others might have considered too difficult to overcome.

Neil's newfound knowledge fueled his creative spirit. He began designing more sophisticated models, incorporating new technologies and bold engineering principles. His designs were not merely replicas; they were ambitious projects, incorporating elements of real-world spacecraft design and functionality. He explored the possibility of incorporating solar sails for propulsion, researched advanced materials for heat shielding, and studied the challenges of long-duration space travel. He even started learning basic coding, envisioning a future where he could contribute to the software development of future space missions.

The "Reaching for the Stars" foundation, which had initially been conceived as a small community initiative, blossomed into a thriving organization. Neil's story had resonated with people worldwide, inspiring countless children and adults to pursue their dreams, regardless of the obstacles they faced. The foundation expanded its reach, offering mentorship programs, STEM workshops, and scholarships to students from underprivileged backgrounds who showed promise in science and technology. Neil's unique perspective, shaped by his own experiences, allowed him to understand and relate to the challenges faced by these young aspirants.

He collaborated with engineers, scientists, and educators, drawing upon their skills to create educational programs that were both informative and engaging. His workshops focused on hands-on learning, encouraging students to experiment, innovate, and develop their problem-solving skills. He emphasized the importance of perseverance, highlighting the fact that failure was not an endpoint, but a stepping stone towards success. He encouraged them to find creative solutions to their challenges, reminding them that limitations were often self-imposed and could be overcome with determination and resourcefulness.

Neil's public appearances became increasingly frequent. He spoke at schools, universities, and international conferences, inspiring audiences with his story of resilience, determination, and unwavering belief in the power of dreams. He emphasized the significance of pursuing one's passions, despite societal expectations or perceived limitations. He stressed the importance of seeking out mentors and support systems, and the power of collaboration in achieving ambitious goals. He became a powerful advocate for inclusive education and equal opportunities, ensuring that children from all backgrounds had the chance to pursue their dreams in STEM fields.

His interactions with aspiring young scientists and engineers deepened his own understanding of the field. He learned about the groundbreaking research being conducted in various areas of space exploration, and he felt a renewed sense of purpose in contributing to this exciting endeavor. He started to envision a future where he might not just be an inspiring figure, but an active participant in space exploration itself. He dreamt of one day designing and building real spacecraft, pushing the boundaries of human knowledge and expanding the reach of humanity's exploration of the cosmos.

Beyond the technical aspects of space exploration, Neil devoted time to understanding the social and ethical implications of space travel. He researched the impact of space exploration on our planet and considered the challenges of sustainability in space. He was mindful of the need to create ethical and responsible guidelines for space exploration, ensuring that the vast resources of space were utilized wisely and equitably. He wanted to ensure that future space endeavors were conducted in a manner that respects the environment and avoids perpetuating existing inequalities.

Neil's future aspirations weren't solely focused on the technological aspects of space exploration. He recognized the crucial role of communication and education in inspiring future generations of scientists and engineers. He started working on a series of children's books meant to simplify complex scientific concepts and spark a love for science and space exploration in young minds. He meticulously crafted stories that were both informative and engaging, incorporating elements of his own journey to make the stories relatable and inspirational.

He also envisioned creating an interactive museum dedicated to space exploration, a place where children could experience the wonder and excitement of space firsthand. The museum would feature hands-on exhibits, simulations, and interactive displays that would bring the universe to life. He aimed to make it a space where children of all backgrounds, abilities, and interests could feel welcome and inspired to explore their own potential.

His journey wasn't just about achieving his personal dreams; it was about building a legacy of hope, inspiration, and inclusivity. He aimed to create a world where every child, regardless of their background or physical abilities, felt empowered to pursue their passions and make their unique contribution to the world. He understood that his own journey had been shaped by the unwavering support of his community, and he wanted to pay that forward, ensuring that others had the same opportunities he had been fortunate enough to receive. The path ahead remained long and full of challenges, but Neil, fueled by his enduring passion and unwavering belief in the power of dreams, was ready to embark on this next phase of his inspiring journey. The journey to the stars was a marathon, not a sprint, and Neil was prepared to run it, with the whole community cheering him on.

CHAPTER 30:

THE ENDURING POWER OF DREAMS

The years that followed were a whirlwind of activity, a testament to Neil's unwavering dedication and the infectious enthusiasm he inspired. His children's books, a vibrant collection titled "Adventures Among the Stars," became instant bestsellers. Each story, meticulously crafted with captivating illustrations, followed a young protagonist who faced enormous odds and still found a way to achieve their dreams. The books weren't just entertaining; they were subtle yet powerful tools, teaching children the importance of resilience, critical thinking, and creative problem-solving. They weren't just about space; they were about the power of believing in yourself, no matter how big or impossible your dream might seem.

Neil's interactive space museum, "Cosmic Wonders," opened its doors to the public to much fanfare. It was a marvel of interactive exhibits, carefully designed to engage children of all ages and abilities. Children could pilot simulated spacecraft, explore virtual lunar landscapes, and learn about the wonders of the universe through hands-on activities. The museum was a testament to Neil's belief in inclusive education, ensuring that every child, regardless of their background or physical limitations, felt welcomed and inspired. He personally led workshops, sharing his experiences and encouraging children to embrace their unique talents. The museum quickly became a renowned center for STEM education, inspiring countless young minds to reach for the stars.

His "Reaching for the Stars" foundation continued to flourish, expanding its programs to reach more children around the world. Neil, now a globally recognized advocate for STEM education and inclusivity, traveled extensively, speaking at conferences,

"

schools, and universities. He shared his inspiring story, not as a tale of achievement alone, but as a testament to the power of believing in oneself, even in the face of adversity. His speeches weren't mere lectures; they were deeply personal narratives that drew listeners in and left them feeling they could take on the world.

He collaborated with leading scientists and engineers on groundbreaking projects, contributing his unique perspective and innovative solutions to complex challenges. His insights, shaped by his own journey of overcoming limitations, proved invaluable. He was no longer just an inspiration; he was an active participant in shaping the future of space exploration. His contributions extended beyond the technical realm; he became a champion for ethical space exploration, advocating for responsible resource management and sustainable practices. He understood that the universe was a shared heritage and that future endeavors must be guided by principles of equity and environmental stewardship.

One particular project stood out: the development of a new generation of prosthetic limbs specifically designed for individuals involved in intricate tasks, like operating sophisticated equipment in space. Drawing on his own experiences and the advancements in prosthetics technology, Neil worked tirelessly with a team of engineers and medical professionals to create a revolutionary device that not only restored functionality but enhanced dexterity and precision. The project, a culmination of his passion for space exploration and his commitment to improving lives, was a resounding success, proving the power of innovation and inclusive design. The prosthetic limb, hailed as a breakthrough in assistive technology, offered new possibilities for individuals with physical differences to pursue their dreams, regardless of physical limitations.

Neil's journey was far from over. He continued to expand his horizons, exploring new avenues of scientific inquiry, and collaborating on ambitious projects that pushed the boundaries of human knowledge and technological innovation. He stayed deeply committed to his foundation, continually seeking ways to empower others and inspire future generations. His life became a living testament to the power of dreams, a beacon of hope illuminating the path for countless individuals who dared to believe they had more to offer than the world expected.

His legacy extended far beyond his accomplishments; it lay in the countless lives he touched, the dreams he ignited, and the opportunities he created. He showed the world that limitations were often self-imposed, and that true potential existed not in the absence of challenges, but in the courage to overcome them. He inspired a generation of young dreamers, reminding them that the journey was just as important as the destination, and that the most rewarding experiences came from embracing the challenges and learning from the setbacks along the way.

The story of Neil is not merely a tale of overcoming adversity; it's a universal narrative of hope and resilience. It is a story of self-belief, unwavering determination, and the transformative power of dreams. It speaks to the inherent human spirit, reminding us that within each of us lies the potential to achieve greatness, regardless of our perceived limitations. Neil's journey continues to inspire and empower, serving as a reminder that the most extraordinary achievements often come from the humblest beginnings and the most unwavering belief in oneself.

His story is a beacon of hope, a testament to the enduring power of the human spirit, and a celebration of the boundless possibilities that lie ahead when we dare to dream big and embrace the journey with courage and determination. It's a reminder that the true measure of success lies not in reaching a predetermined destination, but in the strength of character, the resilience, and the unwavering belief in oneself that are cultivated along the way. It's a message that transcends generations, languages, and cultures; a timeless tale of inspiration and hope that will continue to resonate with readers for years to come.

Neil's story is a call to action, urging readers to embrace their unique talents and pursue their passions with unwavering enthusiasm. It's a reminder that limitations are often perceived, not inherent, and that with perseverance and belief in oneself, even the most seemingly impossible dreams can be realized. His impact extended far beyond his personal achievements; he inspired a global movement, fostering a sense of community and shared purpose among individuals who, like him, dared to dream beyond the confines of what society believed possible.

His story is an ode to the human spirit's ability to transcend limitations, a celebration of the power of dreams to shape our destinies, and a testament to the transformative impact of unwavering belief in oneself. It's a story that invites readers of all ages to reflect on their own aspirations, embrace their unique qualities, and embark on their own extraordinary journeys towards fulfilling their potential. Neil's journey continues to inspire and empower, reminding us that even amidst the challenges and setbacks life inevitably presents, the enduring power of dreams can guide us toward a future filled with hope, accomplishment, and unwavering self-belief. The journey, as Neil so eloquently proved, is the destination, and the true reward lies in the growth, resilience, and unwavering spirit we cultivate along the way. The end of Neil's story is not an ending, but a beginning, the spark for countless other journeys lit by his own.

ACKNOWLEDGMENTS

Writing this book has been a journey filled with joy and learning, and I am deeply grateful to the many individuals who supported me along the way. First, my heartfelt thanks go to my family, whose unwavering encouragement and belief in my work fueled my creativity and kept me going during challenging times. A special thank you to my editor, Peggy, for her insightful guidance and meticulous attention to detail. Her ability helped to shape this story into the best version it could be. To my Mother, Lorelei, who always encouraged my writing and bought me my first typewriter so many years ago. We will meet again.

While this story is fictional, it draws inspiration from the real-life achievements of many individuals who have overcome challenges to pursue their dreams.

Finally, I want to thank all my grandchildren who inspired this story, reminding me of the power of dreams and the enduring spirit of youth. This book is dedicated to you.

AUTHOR BIOGRAPHY

Mr. Annas believes in the power of storytelling to encourage children to embrace their unique talents and pursue their dreams, no matter how challenging they may seem. He is also a firm believer in diversity, inclusivity, and STEM education, advocating for a future where every child feels empowered to reach their full potential. In his spare time, Mr. Annas enjoys stargazing, spending time with family, and dreaming of going into space, if only through this book.